Hilo Dome

Book One

Jack Bartley

Hilo Dome

HistriaYA

Las Vegas ◊ Chicago ◊ Palm Beach

Published in the United States of America by
Histria Books
7181 N. Hualapai Way, Ste. 130-86
Las Vegas, NV 89166 USA
HistriaBooks.com

HistriaYA is an imprint of Histria Books dedicated to incredible books for Young Adult readers. Titles published under the various imprints of Histria Books are distributed worldwide.

All rights reserved. No part of this book may be reprinted or reproduced or utilized in any form or by any electronic, mechanical or other means, now known or hereafter invented, including photocopying and recording, or in any information storage or retrieval system, without the permission in writing from the Publisher.

Library of Congress Control Number: 2024948102

ISBN 978-1-59211-534-1 (softbound)
ISBN 978-1-59211-549-5 (eBook)

Copyright © 2025 by Jack Bartley

For my sons, Colin and Aidan
It took you long enough, Dad!

Prologue

The members of the Ohana family knew the story of Hilo Dome all too well. It had been passed down from generation to generation for over two hundred years. As a young child, Nathan had listened to his grandmother recount how his ancestors had survived the most devastating event in human history, and how the world outside their domed environment had been changed forever.

The nuclear warheads had rained down upon the Earth like a global thunderstorm of fire. The United Domed Cities of the Americas had not willingly entered into the world war. The domes were never intended to withstand such an onslaught. They had been designed primarily to screen out dangerous levels of UV light, the result of a depleted ozone layer from years of pollution, and to raise crops in a controlled environment to avoid the erratic climatic changes, the legacy of global warming. Warheads that exploded close to the domes released enormous amounts of heat, enough to melt even the advanced plastic composites of the protective shields. As the domes melted, they collapsed in on the enclosed cities, encasing them in a molten shroud that re-hardened within minutes after the explosion.

Cities that were not directly affected by the explosions, but were downwind from the blast, suffered longer. The dome air circulators could not filter out the fine radioactive dust particles that drifted in an invisible lethal cloud from the detonation center. Radioactive particles produced radiation sickness that killed thousands within the first few days. Those who did not die immediately slowly died from a variety of diseases that their weakened immune systems were no longer able to fight off. In many cases, the population of an entire dome ceased to exist.

The chaos was inevitable. Communications between domes ceased almost immediately. Relay satellites had also been targeted, and the electromagnetic pulses (EMPs) from the explosions wiped out all forms of television, radio, and interpersonal communicators on the ground. The few cities that were not directly affected by the initial blasts or by radiation became isolated islands, forced to exist without the cooperation of other domed cities. The lack of resources began to slowly strangle the remaining cities.

The distant ancestors of Nathan Ohana's family had been fortunate to live in a dome located on the island of Hawaii, the Big Island, located virtually in the center of the Pacific Ocean. The small domed city of Hilo had escaped the fate of its sister domes on Oahu. The enormous naval presence in Pearl Harbor and the other military bases around Oahu drew missile fire like yellow jackets to a glass of Coke. Fortunately for Hilo, the trade winds carried most of the radiation out to sea, away from the island. The dome structure was enough to shield the inhabitants from the dangers of the light fallout that did drift over from Oahu. Blessed with warm temperatures, ample fresh water, and sunlight, the rich volcanic soil was able to yield enough crops to support the dome population. Hilo was able to avoid the thirst and starvation that slowly strangled many of the other surviving cities.

In spite of the plentiful resources, Nathan, his parents, and the rest of the citizens of Hilo were now facing a new, life-threatening challenge, possibly as dire as the conditions that had threatened the dome centuries ago. Nathan was old enough to recognize that the interruptions in electrical service, recommendations to boil all water before drinking, and the sight of people wearing protective fiber masks over their nose and mouth were becoming more frequent.

Replacement parts for machinery were unavailable, machinery that was necessary to purify the air and water for the dome, and Hilo did not have the industrial capacity to manufacture them. The relatively abundant resources of Hilo were not enough to overcome the mechanical failures of the life support systems as over two hundred years of constant operation pushed the machinery to the edge of collapse.

The conversations he heard about conditions in the dome while in his classes at school, with his friends, and even at home with his parents at the dinner table all pointed to one very disturbing fact: time was running out.

PART 1
Departure

1
Awakening

Nathan peered down into the dark cavern, the home of Talonwrath the Dragon. Or so the local peasants had told him. The rumors and myths in the town below had directed him to follow the Path of Doom, from which no man returns. The people told him in hushed whispers that he would find a series of runes at the end of the path that would describe the ways to align the secret stones, revealing the mouth of the cave. He had solved the puzzle of the secret stones, and the dragon hunt seemed to be going well, except for the smell. It was putrid. It was worse than boiling cabbage, worse than rotten eggs, and even worse than the Mystery Meat served in the school cafeteria. Nathan figured if he could choke that down, he could at least check out the cave a bit further.

He drew Fred, the magical sword that had been given to him by the old crone in the village below. The haggard witch-woman had told him it was the only weapon that could pierce the armor scales of the beast that had plagued the village for centuries. Nathan was slightly annoyed at the name of his magic sword: Fred. Other swords had great names like Excalibur, or even Sting, from *Lord of the Rings*. But no, his sword was Fred. Fred the Magnificent! Fred the Dealer of Death! Nothing worked.

Lacking confidence in his sword's name did not deter him. He began to descend into the dragon's lair when …

"Nathan!"

Someone was calling his name. It sounded far away, like someone searching for him down below in the village. He ignored the voice and turned back to his quest, determined to slay the …

"Nathan!"

It was louder this time, getting closer. Who could it be? Distracted, he turned in the direction of the sound, and as he did, his foot hit some loose rocks at the cave's entrance. They rolled inward, toward the edge of the pit that led down to Talonwrath's lair. The stones rolled over the edge and into the abyss, echoing throughout the cavern as they bounced downward against the walls of the cave toward the fire-lizard.

"Oh man! So much for the element of surprise," Nathan said to himself. It was then that the low rumble rolled over him, like the sound of the loudest machine he had ever heard. The beast was awakening. Nathan's anger welled up inside him. "Who would disturb me at such a sensitive and dangerous time as this? Who would dare to interrupt my quest as I seek to rid the world of this demon? Who placed me in mortal danger as I—"

"NATHAN!"

Mom?

"Nathan Ohana, if you don't get up now and get in here for breakfast, you won't be able to go with me on 'Take Your *Keiki* to Work Day!'"

Nathan sat bolt upright in his bed, leaving the dragon behind while at the same time smacking his head on the goose neck lamp he used for reading at night. *Welcome back to the real world*, he thought. He jumped out of bed as he rubbed his head and looked through the pile of clothes on his floor. After returning several items to the pile after his patented "Sniff-And-Reject" test, he decided to get something clean out of his bureau. He threw on some tan shorts and a purple T-shirt—his favorite. Nathan made it as far as the bedroom door.

"Nathan! You'll need to take a shower if you're going in with me today!"

Moms! Nathan stomped into the bathroom, took off the clothes HE HAD JUST PUT ON, and climbed into the shower. Five seconds later (or so it seemed to his mother), he was drying off and donning the clothes he had just removed.

As he entered the kitchen, his mom said, "What took you so long in the shower?"

Nathan thought, *Why me? How did I get to be the son of the Master of Sarcasm?* He walked over to his stool at the counter where he ate breakfast and stared at the plate. Eggs, again. Eggs, eggs, eggs, eggs! He looked over at his mother, who was standing by the microwave burner. She stared back; her dark brown eyes had the power to penetrate into his brain.

"What's the matter? You like eggs, right?" She paused. "You liked eggs yesterday, and the day before. What's wrong now?"

Silence. Nathan wisely sat down and began to eat his eggs.

"Would you rather have had *poi*? It's certainly easier for me to make. I could just spoon some *lomi lomi kāhala* alongside it, and I'd be done." Lora Ohana sighed and shook her head. Nathan continued to eat, in silence. He would gladly take eggs over the purple-gray library paste *poi*, a substance made from the taro plant that claimed to be actual food.

But he was thinking, *Poi! Kāhala! That's all we ever get, besides chicken.* Nathan knew that fish and chicken were almost the only sources of animal protein for the people of the Hilo Dome. Soybean products added plant-based protein. *Edamame*, the steamed soybean pods, were his favorite because you could squeeze the pods, and the beans would pop right out. He had read about other foods, like beef and pork, but none of them existed in Hilo. In fact, they had not been on a plate in Hilo for over two hundred years. Cows and pigs ate too much food and took up too much room. And, he giggled inwardly, they pooped and farted too much!

Chickens were easy. They ate almost everything and could live just about anywhere. Everyone had them. Chickens were mobile garbage cans that dispensed eggs and could be served up in many different ways. The *kāhala*, a kind of amberjack fish, were farmed in big underwater pens out in Hilo Bay. Nathan knew all about the drone submarines that tended the "farms" since his father was in charge of them. The subs left from an underwater port on Coconut Island off Banyan Drive, close to where Waiakea Pond emptied into Hilo Bay. The drones dispensed chicken bone meal and soybean-based food pellets to the fish and harvested them in old trawler nets that they brought back into a port under the island.

The subs were the only things that ever left the confines of the dome. As far as anyone knew, no person or living thing had left Hilo Dome since the Great War over two hundred years ago. Nothing, not even a stupid chicken. Nathan had heard rumors of giant radioactive beasts living in the forests outside the dome. The word was, if someone or something left the dome, it was a one-way trip.

The Dome was actually a large main dome about four kilometers in diameter connected by arched passageways to three smaller domes on its periphery. These smaller domes housed most of the agricultural areas. Power was provided by water-powered turbines located in the Wailuku River that flowed through the northwest section of the main dome. These turbine generators provided virtually all the power to the domes. The problem was that they were very old, and keeping them running was extremely difficult since there was no way to manufacture replacements for parts that failed. The one exception to this power source was where

Nathan's father worked, at the *kāhala* farm submarine base. Here, power was provided by the only solar panels that still existed, the only ones still functioning after 200 years. The submarines and the guidance systems that enabled the remote harvesting of the *kāhala* ran on electric batteries that were charged by these solar panels.

Nathan pushed his eggs around the plate, mixing the runny yolk with the whites so he would not have to eat them by themselves. *Tasteless rubber*, he thought. He had been hoping that he could go to the port with his father. The sub base, that's where the excitement was! But Nathan's father had told him that it was going to be an extremely busy harvest day down at the port, and that he would have to leave very early. That was all Nathan had to hear. He liked to stay up way too late reading his books to get up early with his father.

Instead, he was going to the office with his mother. Lora Ohana had a very important job with the dome government supervising environmental control. Filtered air circulation throughout the dome was extremely important for keeping the air oxygenated and for temperature control. Even with air circulation, the dome temperature was 10^0 to 20^0 warmer than the outside temperatures. Higher temperatures would make the dome unlivable. Obviously, her job was important; it was just not very exciting.

Of course, anything was better than going to Hilo Middle School, so environmental control it would have to be. It was not that Nathan did not like the subjects taught in his school. He did very well in math and English, especially writing. He figured his writing skill came from all the reading he did. In fact, he truly believed he was running out of books that he had not read. The Hilo Dome library could only stock so many volumes, and very few books were written inside the dome anymore.

When Nathan had really good dreams, he tried to write them out as soon as he could so the details wouldn't be lost, like the one last night about the dragon. Now he could not even remember the dragon's name, and his vision of the cave was disappearing. Nathan suddenly jumped when he realized his mother's face was just inches from his, her elbows resting on the counter.

"Hello! Earth to Nathan!" Lora stood up. "If you're finished, go brush your teeth, and try to do something with that hair. Perhaps a comb?"

Sarcasm. Again. *What else would I use, an old fish skeleton?* Nathan took his plate over to the sink, rinsed it, and put it in the automatic dishwasher. He thought that it was a good thing his father knew how to fix things or else he would be washing the dishes himself. The machine was probably as old as his father, maybe older, but it worked. Well, it worked most of the time.

He ran to the bathroom, brushed his teeth, and attacked his thick, sandy blond hair with his comb. The hair was winning. Quick, get some water! There, it's down. It's up. Comb, comb, comb. It's down. Sprong, it's up again. Once again, the hair emerged victorious. Nathan gave up. He thought, *Where did I get this stuff? Mom and Dad have nice, obedient, shiny black hair.* He stared at the mirror. *And my eyes; they're green, not dark brown like my parents.* In fact, he often thought about the fact that he did not look like his parents. Not only that, he did not look like anyone else in his school.

Nathan figured that his appearance might be the cause of some of his social problems at school. Even though he did well in his classes, Nathan simply did not have many friends, and those he did have were not exactly the most popular kids in school. In fact, his group of friends was often the subject of ridicule and hurtful jokes. As much as he liked his friends, Nathan really wanted to be able to fit in, to "hang" with whomever he wanted. He did not like the feeling that he was on the outside.

Nathan had his reading and writing to help console him when he felt lonely, but most of all, it was playing his guitar that was best at helping him leave his troubles behind. It was his most prized possession. The beautiful *koa* wood instrument had belonged to his grandfather, a man Nathan had never met. He felt like he knew him from all the stories his mother had told about him. She would share these stories with him as she taught him the basics of how to play. If only he had some friends to play along with him. Nathan sighed and turned away from the curiosity he saw reflected in the mirror.

He walked into the kitchen as his mother was packing up her *kapa* cloth bag with things for work. Most of his clothes were made from the same coarse material, pounded and pressed out from paper mulberry bark, then dyed with red and brown extracts from other plants and the volcanic soil. Because of this, just about all the clothes and cloth materials looked very much alike. That is why Nathan liked his purple T-shirt so much. The purple color cost a little more because it was made from grapes. *It was worth it*, he thought, *even though it stained my neck purple the first few times I wore it.*

Lora Ohana finished packing her things and looked up at Nathan. "Nice job with the hair. Let's go or I'll be late for my first meeting." Nathan grabbed a couple of books and an old-fashioned set of maze puzzles and threw them in his backpack since there would be long periods of time when his mother would be locked up in meetings. Being left alone was okay; it was better than being in school! Nathan and his mother climbed on their bicycles for the short ride over to her office. Anticipating boredom, Nathan could not have known that what he would learn in the next few hours would change his life forever.

***

Outside the dome, not far from Nathan, and just up the coast in the small village of Honoli'i, Kayli Pahinui stood at the counter in the kitchen, scooping seeds out of her breakfast papaya. She wanted to save the seeds from this one because this particular fruit was very large, smelled sweet, and had the brightest red-orange color she had ever seen. They were easy to grow in the rich volcanic soil that her village was built upon, and these seeds would be a good start for her own small orchard. It gave her some joy in this otherwise gloomy morning.

Kayli had planned to go on a hunting expedition at the request of Edward Park, the village butcher. He had told her that many people in the village had been requesting more Kahlij pheasant for their dinner tables, and Kayli knew just the spot to find them. They were very plentiful in a clearing in the forest not far from Honoli'i after expanding their range over hundreds of years from the upper parts of Mauna Loa and Mauna Kea. It would be an all-day round trip, but she had done it many times before.

At fourteen, Kayli was extremely independent and very skilled with the longbow and crossbow. People said that she was a better shot than even Aaron or Byl, her two older brothers. Taking after her father, Sam Pahinui, Kayli was tall for her age, taller than most of the girls two or three years older than she was. Her wiry strength came from years of working the family farm with her mother, Layla, and her Auntie Bernice, and fishing from the family's outrigger canoes with her two brothers. Paddling the *wa'a kaukahi* through the surf and into the open ocean was not an easy task. Her parents had no problem with her going on these short hunting trips, and Edward Park had come to rely on her skills to keep his shop well stocked. She often came back with a small *pua'a*, the wild pigs that were almost as common as the pheasants.

One problem. Before her father left their *hale* on his way to work, he had told her that she needed to help her mother and Auntie Bernice move the goats from their current pen to a new one in a better grazing area, and then had to tend to the *taro* patch, harvesting some of the leaves before the tubers were to be dug up about two weeks from now. Kayli knew it was an important job; *taro* provides greens, a starchy root that can be cooked, flour for baking, and of course, *poi*. When left to ferment, "three-finger" *poi* was her father's favorite condiment. Kayli did not like to disappoint her father.

However, working the family farm for the day meant that she would have to postpone her hunting trip until the following day. As she thought about it, Kayli tried to see the bright side of remaining in the village for the day. A light rain was expected today, but tomorrow was predicted to be clear and sunny, and she preferred hunting in good weather. The paths from the village and through the forest were very slippery when they were wet.

Kayli scooped out her first bite of papaya, thinking about her plans for the following day. The weird thing about going to the clearing was that it was close to the dome. Kayli often wondered what life would be like in such a confined area, never getting soaked by the warm rain, feeling the trade winds that were a constant in her life, or riding the waves into the beach after catching some fish for dinner. Experiencing all these things, and much more, was freedom, not confinement. Although many in the village resented the people of Hilo for locking them out when the dome closed, shutting them out before the war, she was grateful. As far as she was concerned, the dome could stay closed forever.

2
Revelation

It was a short bike ride, about three kilometers, from the Ohana home on Kalanikoa Street to the office buildings that housed the various government agencies that kept the dome operational. The bike ride was safe because there were no motor vehicles in the dome, and it was always a dry ride since it never "rained," except by directed spray in some of the agricultural areas, like the *taro* field located in what was formerly the Hilo airport.

The Hilo Environmental Control Office was housed with all the other government offices in an ancient two-story structure that used to be The Federal Building and was relatively close to the port where Nathan's father worked. Nathan and his mother coasted down Kalanikoa Street to Kamehameha Bikeway, the wide path named after the ancient ruler who united the Hawaiian Islands that ran along the bay front. Even though he couldn't get out to the bay, the view through the dome was something Nathan always enjoyed. Nathan tried to imagine what Kamehameha would think of his islands today. He was sure the old king would be heartbroken to know that most of Hawaii, along with the rest of the world, had been poisoned by radioactive fallout from the Great War.

Nathan and his mother turned up Waianuenue Street, pedaled a couple of blocks uphill, and stuck their bikes in the rack outside the main entrance. Most of the old buildings here were only two stories, so they walked up to Lora's second-floor office. Nathan was aware of many conversations going on around him, even though he could not actually hear them through the walls and closed doors. This was because his sandy hair and green eyes were not the only features that were special about him.

From birth, Nathan could not speak due to a genetic problem that left him without a functional larynx, his voice box. His parents could understand Nathan because they had found a book about American Sign Language in the library, so from the time Nathan should have been able to talk, he communicated with his parents using ASL.

Not being able to talk caused Nathan all kinds of problems, but he had one other genetic anomaly that was bestowed upon him as if it were to compensate for his inability to talk. In his mind, Nathan could interpret the thoughts of other people and mentally perceive conversations of people from as far away as one hundred meters. Only his parents were aware of this special ability, and even they did not know just how acute his unique sensory perception was.

Nathan was not quite sure how he was able to pick up other people's thoughts when they were thinking and talking, but sometimes it seemed to be a curse more than a gift. He often intercepted conversations his parents had that they thought were secret. From these discussions, he knew that both of them were concerned about the deteriorating conditions of the dome and that the people in charge of the dome were taking actions that did not seem to be fair or democratic. His parents usually seemed cheerful when he was with them, but at times, he knew they were terribly upset and depressed by the conditions in Hilo and the people who were their bosses.

Nathan also knew that it was not his appearance that really caused him to be ostracized at school; it was the fact that he could not speak. His inability to talk, combined with his unusual appearance, made him feel like a freak, even though he knew he was very intelligent, and, despite his lack of speech, he did very well in his classes. Getting some of the best grades in the entire school probably did not help his social status, either, and he would often lie awake in his bed, unable to sleep, trying to decide if he should "dumb it down" just to be less conspicuous. Nathan found that he could not bring himself to do that, even if it might help him to fit in.

As soon as they entered the small room that served as an office, Lora settled in behind her computer. Nathan found an uncomfortable chair in a corner by the door, the only other chair besides the one at the computer desk, and opened one of the books he pulled from his backpack. It was a well-worn copy of *Enders Game* that he never tired of reading. Lora watched him settle in and said, "I'll be here for about another thirty minutes, then I have a meeting to go to that may last until lunch. You'll be okay while I'm gone, right? You can use my computer, if you want." Nathan nodded and turned his attention back to his book.

He thought, *Use her computer? What good is that?* Nathan knew that, before the Great War, computers could talk to each other all over the world through some kind of communications net. His mother's computer only connected to a few others in the government building, the only ones that still functioned in Hilo besides the controllers at the sub base. It was fun to type out his stories on it, but that is about all it was good for as far as he was concerned.

Unfortunately, Nathan could not concentrate on his book, even though he usually found it to be fascinating. He kept picking up a rather heated discussion going on somewhere in the building, an argument about failed systems in the dome and possibly turning to the outside to replenish dwindling resources. He thought, *The outside? How can anyone survive on the outside?* His mental eavesdropping was interrupted by his mother's departure.

"I'll be back by lunch," Lora said as she went out the door. She smiled and added, "Don't get into trouble." Nathan rolled his eyes and nodded again, then tried to get back into his story as the door closed behind his mother. However, the more he tried to concentrate on the story, the more details he "heard" from the discussion somewhere in the building. Nathan could make out that they were talking about not having enough food for the dome population due to equipment failures and not enough materials to construct places to live or repair the failing machinery. When the subject of a feral population of humans existing outside the dome came up, he put the book down and gave up on trying to read. People living outside the dome? No one had ever mentioned such a possibility. Monsters, yes, but people, no. Now, as his concentration shifted entirely to the conversation, the voices became more distinct.

"We'll have to deal with them. We know the Ferals are out there, and I seriously doubt that they'll give up land, food, and other resources very readily," said one of the voices.

"I know that, Mr. Mayor, but we don't even know what they're like, or how they've, um, changed or mutated after possibly getting dosed with all that radiation. They may even harbor that Ebola Hemorrhagic Flu that swept across the globe just before the war started." The voice paused. "We also don't know if they're still pissed at us for shutting them out of the dome when the Great War started. They could still harbor some pretty hostile feelings toward us, even after two centuries. We need to be prepared to, shall we say, neutralize them. In fact, I think we should proceed along those lines rather aggressively."

Nathan was startled. The mayor! He was intercepting a private conversation with the person who was in charge of the Hilo Dome government. Roy Hapuna had been elected to serve as mayor over twenty years ago, way before Nathan was born. Elections were supposed to happen every five years, but Hapuna, along with his Chief of Security, had declared a state of emergency and suspended the democratic process. Nathan knew his parents still had their jobs because they did what they were told and did not openly question what was happening in Hilo. He had also heard that some who did voice their opposition to government operations had lost their jobs, or as rumors implied, simply disappeared. The kids at school even suggested that the bodies of the "disappeared" were ground up and fed to the *kāhala*, a proposition hotly denied by Nathan since that implied his father had something to do with it. However, it was for that reason that Nathan did not like the sound of the term "neutralizing" that was suggested by the second voice.

"I'm afraid you might be right, Chief. Our dome is basically a small "island" on a remote island with limited resources, and our tests now show that it should be safe for us to go out there, outside the dome, for at least limited amounts of time. We need to be prepared not only to defend ourselves against the Ferals and any diseases they may carry, but to possibly take what we think is necessary for the people of Hilo. It's either that or we have to find ways to start reducing the population of Hilo more directly. Some sort of euthanization policy might be in order."

The population of Hilo was already tightly controlled. In an enclosed environment like a dome, there was no way to expand agriculture, and there was no way to increase vital resources, such as water. The people of Hilo faced very strict rules about how many children a family could have. Each year, the government would tally how many people had died during that year. That would be the number of children that could be born in the following year. Who got to reproduce was determined by a lottery; the families with no children were in the first "pool" of the lottery. If there were many deaths in one year, then a second "pool" of families was established from couples with just one child. If they did not conceive in their allotted year, they got a "pass" to try again the following year. It was very rare to see a family with three children. Oddly enough, Mayor Hapuna and Chief of Security, Howard Teshima, were the fathers of such families.

Nathan could not believe this discussion was taking place between the mayor and the chief of Hilo Dome security. His first thought was that it would be totally wrong to just assume that the feral people (Ferals?) needed to be "neutralized," a term he assumed meant to wipe them out. He really was not sure how this could be done. He had never seen a serious weapon carried by anyone. There was no hunting in the dome, and everybody knew everyone. People never even locked their doors. Most households and a few shops had knives for preparing food, but Nathan could not imagine going out into the wilds outside the dome and attacking the Ferals with just those kinds of weapons.

And what did they mean about "reducing the population of Hilo" or euthanization? It was already controlled. Would they limit births even more? Would they euthanize people after a certain age or if they were terminally ill?

He had to let his parents know just what he had learned. Nathan got up out of his chair and searched around his mother's desk for a piece of paper and a pencil and began to take notes.

3
Discovered

After what seemed like hours of notetaking, Nathan was startled when his mother stuck her head into the office and said, "Sorry, Nathan, I know I said I'd only be in the meeting until lunch, but it's running a lot longer than I expected. Here's some money. You don't mind going out to get something on your own, do you?" Nathan shook his head, took the money, and then pointed to the notes he had been writing.

"I can't read that right now, Nathan. I really have to get back to the meeting. I'm sure it's very creative, though." Nathan thought she seemed a little distracted. "I'll read it as soon as I get back. Okay?" Before Nathan could issue any kind of protest, Lora disappeared from the doorway.

I guess it can wait until after lunch, Nathan thought. He was terribly upset by the conversation, but for now, there was nothing he could do about it. He felt very frustrated that he had to sit on something that he thought was important, even for a short period of time. His feelings diminished his appetite, but dinner was a long way off. At least there was a good take-out place a couple of blocks down from the office building. He sighed and reluctantly put his notes, along with his book, on his mother's desk.

Nathan made his way down the stairs and out of the building without intercepting any other conversations. He was deep in thought as he walked slowly down the street, but as he turned the corner, the vision of the L & L Drive In made him forget about Ferals and other problems, at least just a little bit. The aromas that drifted out of the restaurant awakened his hunger.

The L & L had been around *forever*. Literally. This institution was a true survivor from the days before the dome existed. It was still called the "Drive In" even though cars had been non-existent for the last two centuries, and the building in which the restaurant was housed had gone through several reincarnations over the years. With or without cars, good food and generous servings were a hard combination to beat. He went in and placed his order by pointing at the menu. Watching the other customers get their food made him realize just how famished he really was; he could not wait until they served up his plate lunch for him. He had ordered it with chicken long rice because it tasted good, and he really liked the fact that the noodles reminded him of snot, great for grossing out the girls at lunch.

Nathan picked up his containers at the counter and paid the cashier. He looked in the bag to make sure they had put in a fork and not chops sticks. There was no way he wanted to battle the slippery noodles without the benefit of what he considered a modern utensil. As Nathan left the L & L, he thought about sitting in the small park across the street but decided instead that he had better get back to the office so he could be there as soon as his mother got out of her meeting. The conversation he had intercepted was starting to work its way back into his mind.

***

At the same time Nathan was leaving for lunch, the mayor dismissed his chief of security, telling him they would pick up on their discussion later in the afternoon. There were more pressing and immediate problems on his plate, and they involved environmental issues. He had to see Lora Ohana about the deteriorating condition of the processing plants that purified water and filtered and re-circulated air for the dome.

The air handlers were in desperate need of preventive maintenance, and the water purifiers were strained to capacity. If the purifiers should fail, waterborne parasites such as *Giardia* and *Cryptosporidium* could cause severe illness throughout the dome, and even death in infants or the very old. *Of course*, Hapuna thought to himself, *that would be one way to reduce the dome population*. He made a mental note to bring it up with Teshima when they met later in the day. He also thought that he could possibly let Lora Ohana take the fall for the spread of the debilitating diseases, even though finding repair parts for the aging systems was really beyond her control. The general public wouldn't need to know. Why not shift the blame?

The mayor got up from his chair with a great deal of effort. With over two hundred and fifty pounds being carried on his five-foot, eight-inch frame, the dome's filters weren't the only things being strained. He walked slowly down the long hallway to Lora Ohana's office, still going over the disease possibilities in his head.

The door to Lora's office was open slightly, so he tapped lightly on the frame. "Lora? Have you got a minute? I need to talk to you about the air and water situation." No response. He pushed the door open a bit and looked around the edge. "Lora?"

It was obvious that no one was there; the office was not that big. The mayor opened the door the rest of the way and squeezed past the chair Nathan had been sitting in. As he stood behind Lora's computer chair, he took a quick look around. Thinking that he would have to catch up with her later, he turned to leave. It was then that he saw the handwritten notes that Nathan had left behind. Leaning over for a better look, it did not take Hapuna long to realize that it was basically a shorthand version of the conversation he had just completed with his chief of security.

"So, it seems we have a spy in our midst, or at least someone nosy enough to cause problems," he said to the empty office. What he could not figure out was how Lora had intercepted his discussion with Teshima just moments earlier. In fact, he was sure Ohana had been in a meeting with her staff for most of the morning. Hapuna looked back at the desk and noticed a book that had been under the notes. Hapuna thought, *This doesn't look like something Lora would be reading.* It was then that he remembered that Lora had asked permission to bring her son in on "Take Your *Keiki* to Work Day." Hapuna had thought it was a stupid idea at the time, and now it appeared to be more than stupid. This kid could expose everything. He tried to think back if he had ever seen Lora's son, and all he could remember was that he had blond hair. Hapuna found the intercom on Lora's desk and pressed the button for Howard Teshima's office.

As soon as he heard Teshima respond, he said, "Howard, meet me in my office. Immediately."

***

As Nathan walked the few blocks back to the office building, a sense of dread began to build inside him. What would happen if he did tell his parents? What could they do about it, and if they did something, what if they were "disappeared?" He climbed the steps to the main entrance and was struck by the silence. No conversations. Not just from the mayor's office, but from virtually the whole building. There was almost always a "buzz" in his mind from remote sources, but now he heard nothing. *I guess everyone went out for lunch*, he thought.

Nathan nodded to the guard on duty as he passed through the main door and climbed the steps to his mother's office. Even though outwardly nothing seemed out of place, he began to move more slowly, as though he expected to find someone waiting for him as he made the turn on the landing. When he found no one waiting to pounce on him there, he figured the next ambush site would be his mother's office. Trying to subdue his paranoia, he slowly and cautiously placed one foot in front of the other as he made his way down the hall. His brain was now working overtime, and the silence closed in on him as he pushed gently on the office door and peeked inside.

4
Ambush

Empty.

Nathan looked around and thought it appeared as though his mother had not yet returned from her meeting. He walked over to her desk to retrieve his notes. Immediately, he could see the papers were missing. Nathan's stomach churned, and he had not even eaten his chicken long rice. His book was there, but no notes, and he was certain that he had placed them on the desk next to the computer. He stood quietly, listening.

Down the hallway in the mayor's office, Lora Ohana sat in a straight-backed wooden chair facing both Hapuna and Teshima. During Nathan's trip to the L & L, they had hauled Lora out of her meeting on the pretext of an emergency problem with the dome air supply. Once inside the office, Teshima ordered Lora to sit in the chair, and they presented her with Nathan's work. It did not take long for Lora to realize that Nathan had stumbled upon something important, and more critically, dangerous.

Hapuna said, "Apparently, your son has gotten a little too nosy for his own good. What's he doing, sneaking around eavesdropping on official conversations? I don't think that's the intent of 'Take Your *Keiki* to Work Day!'"

As Hapuna grilled Lora about the notes, she tried to answer his questions while simultaneously keeping an eye on Teshima. She tried to remain calm in front of Hapuna, but her heart raced as she realized that Teshima was on the phone to his security forces setting a trap for Nathan upon his return. She knew the fear was reflected in her eyes when Hapuna turned to see where her gaze was riveted. He turned back to her with a satisfied, yet evil, grin on his face.

"There's nothing you can do at this point, Lora." Hapuna paused and looked back at Teshima. "So, it would be in everyone's best interests for you to cooperate. We need to, shall we say, *question* Nathan about exactly what it was that he heard, and what he thinks it means."

Teshima hung up the phone and said, "Everything's in place, boss. All we have to do is say the word to spring the trap. The kid should be back from lunch now and up in Lora's office. I'll check to make sure with the guard at the door. Once we know he's in, you just have to give me the word."

In his mother's office, Nathan could now hear Hapuna and Teshima, but he could not quite make out what they were discussing. Instinctively, he edged closer to the door, hoping that it would help his reception of their discussion, even though he knew walls and doors had little effect on thought transmission. Just as he was peeking around the doorway and into the hall, his mother's voice screamed into his brain, "NATHAN! RUN! There's a trap by the security force! The stairs and doors may be guarded."

To Hapuna, Lora still seemed intimidated. He was unaware that she had just transmitted a warning, loud and clear, to Nathan without actually voicing it out loud. To him, at this point, what Lora did was irrelevant, because just as she sent her message, Hapuna turned away from her and gave the order to Teshima to close in on the boy.

Nathan raced out of his mother's office and down the hall. He looked around frantically for a place to escape or hide, but nothing presented itself. As he approached the end of the hallway, he heard multiple sets of footsteps pounding up the stairs. Desperate, Nathan ducked into a bathroom and locked the door.

Great, Nathan thought to himself sarcastically. *They'll never look here.*

Nathan knew he did not have much time, and there were very few places to hide. He could go into the toilet stall and stand on the seat, but that would only work for a few seconds. Great trick in middle school when playing hide-and-seek with your friends, but the security forces would not hesitate to kick in the stall door.

He noticed a small window next to the sink. Nathan yanked at the bottom half of the window and thought his shoulders would pop out of their sockets when the window refused to budge. The window had been painted shut, but he thought the paint looked old and cracked. The footsteps in the hall were slowing down but drawing near. He smacked the lower part of the window frame with the palm of his hand and jiggled the latches. He pushed upwards against the upper part of the frame, and this time, the window lurched open.

The view was disheartening. The bathroom faced the back of the building, but there was no tree to jump on to, and the height was too far to jump from without breaking an ankle or wrist upon landing. He was about to close the window when he heard the guards try the door. The doorknob rattled but held.

Nathan looked out the window again and then noticed an old, corroded downspout that collected and funneled rainwater from the roof before there was a dome. It was clamped to the exterior wall by a series of metal bands and ran all the way down to the ground. *It's my only chance*, he thought. He climbed out the window, kneeled on the broad sill, and tried not to look down. Nathan stretched his arm as far as he dared and grasped the pipe. He could hear the guards pounding on the door. The lock would give at any second.

The next part would be tricky, and one slip would end his escape in an awkward fall to the ground over two stories below, but there was no turning back. Nathan leaned over and grabbed the downspout with his other hand, pushed off the sill with both feet, and swung over so that his knees now straddled the pipe. He started to slip downward, braking with his hands and knees, while the old structure creaked and groaned under his weight. He began to inch his way down when a screeching pop made him look up.

Just above his head, one of the old fasteners holding a clamp into the wall pulled free from the stucco. He would have to hurry, or the whole structure would soon give way. He continued his descent until he was just level with the top of the window of the bathroom on the first floor. Nathan felt sure he could make it down from here. However, at that point, his luck ran out as two other clamps tore loose entirely, and the downspout parted company with the wall it had been hugging for over two hundred years. Pieces of dried stucco rained down on him as the pipe slowly swung out over the grass below.

The downspout began to twist at a point just below the first-floor window where one clamp stubbornly decided that it was going to keep on doing its job. As Nathan pivoted in the air to face the ground, he realized that he would have to make a decision very quickly. If he continued to hold on to the downspout, he would land with his weight on the back of his hands and wrists. Not good.

As the ground rushed up to meet him, Nathan released his hold on the downspout and extended his hands out in front of him, a reflexive move more than a conscious decision. As the spout collided with the ground, Nathan felt the pressure on his wrists and knees as he, too, made a landing. His elbows folded, and his forehead smacked squarely down on the pipe. Stunned, Nathan rolled off the downspout and held his head. He was amazed that you really do see stars when you take a shot to the head.

"There he is!"

Nathan pulled his hands away from his head and looked up at the window he had just left. The security guard that had been pointing down in his direction pulled back from the window. Nathan could hear some shouting from inside the building, and he knew that he had to get moving as quickly as possible. He looked down at his hands and was somewhat surprised to see blood. He touched his forehead again and could feel that it was wet and sticky. Nathan looked at his hand again and was relieved to see that very little additional blood was there. *Can't be too bad*, he thought.

He felt a little woozy as he got to his feet, but his sense of urgency quickly erased any trace of nausea. Nathan ran around the corner of the building so that he was no longer in view from the bathroom window. With his back flat against the wall, he tried to assess what his next course of action should be. He knew the neighborhood like the back of his hand, probably much better than anyone in the security force. There were some old, abandoned buildings that he and his friends used to play in near the bridge that spanned the Wailuku River. They might be the best place to lay low for a while and to figure out what to do next. Whatever action he was going to take, Nathan knew he had to do it immediately. He pictured the route he would need to take in his head.

Nathan left the cover of the building and darted out to the sidewalk that bordered Kinoole Street. When he reached the walkway, he looked back and saw the security forces coming out of the side entrances of the building he had just fled. It would only be a few seconds before they spotted him. As he tried to cross Kinoole to get over to Wailuku Drive, his route to the river, several people on bikes had to swerve to avoid hitting him. When they yelled at him to be more careful, it drew the attention of the guards.

Nathan made it across Kinoole and headed for the abandoned buildings by the bridge. He stayed close to the store fronts, making it harder for the guards to get a good look at him as he darted around startled pedestrians. His next challenge was to get across Wailuku Drive to get on to Wainaku Street, the one with the old buildings and bridge, without being seen. A slight curve at the end of Kinoole would hide him until just before he had to make his final dash.

As he rounded the bend in Kinoole, Nathan froze. Coming up Wailuku Drive were several guards on bicycles. If he remained exposed, they could spot him at any time. Nathan could see the beginning of Wainaku Street, and without giving it a second thought, he sprinted across Wailuku. The guards shouted to each other as they saw Nathan cross the road, but when they turned on to Waianku Street, Nathan had disappeared. The guards could see the old bridge a short distance down the road, but no kid.

Looking through a dusty window from his hiding place in an old aluminum Quonset hut, Nathan could see three guards dismount from their bikes. He could make out from their discussion that they planned to spread out to start an inspection of the row of abandoned huts and buildings that lined the road leading to the bridge. What made his blood run cold was that they also were speaking into radio handsets to let the rest of the guards know that they thought they had him trapped. Also, they had pulled their night sticks. They obviously meant business. Nathan's hopes began to dim as he realized how serious the situation had become.

Nathan realized his only chance to eventually get back to his parents was to get across the bridge to a part of Hilo that used to be called Akina Park, a recreational area now overgrown due to limited resources and neglect. It was even more deserted than where he was at that moment. He could make his way down an old path that used to be Ohai Street and finally get back into town over the lower bridge on Keawe Street. The more he thought about it, the more futile the whole plan sounded, but it was the only option open to him. With guard reinforcements on the way and no time to lose, Nathan made his way to the back of the hut, looking for a way out.

The dim light inside the hut made it difficult to see, and more than once, Nathan tripped over old furniture and equipment that seemed to reach out of the darkness to grab his leg or rise up from the dusty floor to snare his feet. Just as he thought he was almost to the back of the hut, a spider web wrapped around his head, sending him into an arm-waving frenzy in an attempt to get it off. Nathan panicked as his arachnophobia took over, and even though it felt like he was free of the web, he thought the pounding of his heart could be detected by the guards out on the street. It took several minutes of slow, deep breathing to get him calm enough to continue.

After what seemed like hours since the spider ambush, Nathan could make out the back wall of the building, but no door. Feeling trapped once again, Nathan eased his way along the back wall, feeling his way to the side. He could sense that the guards were coordinating their search, but they did not seem to be close to his hut. Not yet.

As he approached the side wall, he could see a shaft of light coming from a thin triangular crack where the corrugated aluminum of the curved top had separated from the back wall. Nathan crouched down to get a closer look. It was not wide enough to get through, but a tentative push on the side gave him some hope; the wall moved. He pushed harder, but a low creaking sound as the old metal started to bend made him freeze. Nathan held his breath for a moment, slowly released his pressure on the side wall, then pressed his hands against the back wall. It began to bend outward without protest. Just as he began to believe he had found his exit, the wall's outward progress stopped, as if blocked by something on the outside.

Maintaining his pressure on the aluminum, Nathan assessed the situation. The crack was almost big enough to squeeze through, and both the side and the back would probably give way enough to let him out. However, the side would most likely cry out again, and he had no idea what he would find the other side. Was it worth the risk? The sound of someone working the metal latch on the front door of the hut made the decision for him. Kneeling, Nathan put his hands in front of his head and pushed through the crack just as the guard stepped inside.

Luckily for Nathan, when the guard heard the groaning aluminum, the guard moved towards the sound. He did not realize it was the farewell cry of his prey escaping the trap. By the time the guard reached the back wall, Nathan was making his way along the back side of the row of Quonset huts, peering around the end wall of each one before making the jump to the cover of the next. Within minutes, Nathan was at the river.

The water roared about thirty feet below him as it raced for Hilo Bay. All Nathan had to do was head upstream while sticking close to the side of the final Quonset hut, cross the bridge, and disappear into the overgrowth on the far side. Staying as low to the ground as possible, Nathan crawled towards the escape route. When he finally reached the front end of the last Quonset hut, Nathan stretched out flat on the ground and gave himself a peek down Wainaku Street towards town.

No one. To his total amazement, Nathan could not see anyone on the street. Cautiously, he stood up and looked across the bridge. It was clear. Without hesitation, Nathan bolted across the bridge for the far side. He was halfway across when he saw two guards on bikes turn the corner from the Ohia path on to Wainaku and head for the bridge. The escape route was blocked. There was no way he could make it over the bridge before they arrived, so he turned to head back. He heard the guards on the bikes call to the original pursuers, and instantly two of them emerged from Quonset huts, cutting off his escape.

Nathan was out of choices and out of escape routes. As the guards closed in, he looked over the edge of the bridge. He felt a little dizzy watching the water as it churned its way from the waterfall far upstream to its exit out of the dome at the edge of the bay. With several days of heavy rain outside the dome, the river was moving more swiftly than he had ever seen it move before. With the guards just ten yards away on either side, he clambered up on the guard rail of the bridge and steadied himself by holding onto one of the supports. With one last look back at his pursuers, Nathan turned to the river and jumped.

5
Down and Out

Howard Teshima set the radio down on the table. He did not look up immediately, but when he did, the concerned look on his face prompted a question from Hapuna. "Well, you do have him, don't you?"

"Um, no, we don't have him." He looked nervously at Lora. "In fact, we don't know exactly where he is."

"How can you not know where he is?" Hapuna was fuming. He heaved himself out of his chair and leaned right into Teshima's face. "Your last report said you had him cornered in the old Quonset huts. How could you not know where he is?"

"Actually, he escaped from the hut he was in and made his way to the bridge over the river. We had men at each end of the bridge. They had him trapped." Teshima paused and backed away from Hapuna ever so slightly.

"Please continue," urged Hapuna, adding sarcastically, "I can't wait to hear how this ends."

Teshima looked back again at Lora. "He jumped. Before they could close in and grab him, the boy climbed on the edge and jumped."

Lora leapt from her chair with a look of horror on her face and screamed at Teshima. "What? How could something like that happen? You had your men chasing a fourteen-year-old kid all over Hilo, and for what? To have him jump off a bridge?" Tears began to pour down her face. "You better have your entire squad of goons down along that river trying to rescue him. If anything happens to him, this whole town will—"

"Will what, Lora?" Hapuna walked slowly over to Lora, placed his hands on her shoulders, and sat her back down in the chair. She was sobbing now but stared defiantly back at Hapuna. "Please continue. I really would like to know what this town will do. It is, after all, my job to know what this town will do." An insincere smile spread across his face.

Lora ignored his question. "I need to call my husband."

"Later," said Hapuna as he turned away from her.

"I need to call him now," Lora insisted.

Hapuna whirled around and leaned over so his face was directly in front of hers. "The only thing you need to do now is calm down and keep this to yourself. In fact," he said as he turned to Teshima, "why don't you have Mrs. Ohana escorted downstairs where she can, shall we say, 'recover' from this traumatic event."

Teshima spoke briefly into the radio and listened for the response. He said to Hapuna, "Two of my men will be here in a minute."

Hapuna remained silent for a moment and then walked slowly back to his chair. As he was sitting down, he said, "Have your men at the bridge fan out along the river downstream from the bridge. Look for places that would be a likely spot for someone to come ashore, especially where the river widens before it gets to the edge of the dome and empties into the bay." When seated, he looked at Lora. "Can your kid swim?"

When he did not receive a response, he raised his voice and asked again, "Can your kid swim?"

Lora looked up slowly. "Yes, he can swim, but he's never been in a river before. I don't know if he can handle the current. As you know, it rained heavily last night. We had to send an inspection team to the point where the river enters the dome just this morning to make sure there were no obstructions against the protective grating." Tears began to stream down her face. "They said … They said the river was as high as they had ever seen it."

At that moment, two security guards appeared in the doorway to the office. Teshima took them out to the hallway, spoke to them briefly, then brought them back inside. "Mrs. Ohana, these two young men will show you to a more comfortable room downstairs where you can wait until we have more news."

Resigned to her fate, Lora stood up, and without looking at either Hapuna or Teshima, left the office with the guards. After they were down the hallway, Hapuna said to Teshima, "Make sure the door is locked once she's in the room. I knew putting that furnished holding cell downstairs would come in handy at some time." Several years earlier, Hapuna had put in a small lounge area, ostensibly for the benefit of the government employees. No one except Hapuna and Teshima knew that a special security door that could be locked from the outside had also been part of the lounge design.

"I'll see to it, Mayor." Teshima left the office to catch up with the guards and their "guest."

***

The security guards fanned out along both sides of the river, concentrating on slight bends in the shoreline and riffle areas where someone might climb out on their own or be washed ashore by the strong current. The heavy rain outside the dome had swollen the river and turned it muddy brown, making it impossible to see anything below the surface. It was tedious work, and in many places, required hacking away dense vegetation with machetes.

In addition to being tedious, it was also dangerous. One guard had already been lost to the swirling currents when he slipped off an embankment and disappeared in the murky waters. The fact that other guards saw the man fall and were still unable to rescue him virtually dimmed all hope they had for a safe recovery of Nathan. The lieutenant in charge of the search team was reluctant to call Teshima. The chief of security was not accustomed to negative reports, and officers who failed to accomplish an assigned task more often than not were relieved of their commission, a fact that drove the lieutenant to push his men even harder in their search.

Finally, after several hours of grueling work, every inch of the river's edge had been covered by the rescue team. It became evident to all involved that a continuation of the search would be futile. A sense of dread gripped the lieutenant as he activated the transmitter of his radio to file his report with Teshima, and as expected, after filing the report, he was ordered to appear before Teshima without delay. The lieutenant hoped that a demotion would be the least of his worries. Little did he know that, as far as Teshima was concerned, not recovering the boy was for the better.

***

When Nathan hit the water, the impact forced every bit of air from his lungs, and the swirling water felt like a huge vacuum was sucking on his legs, pulling him straight down. Just when he thought he would lose consciousness, the current swirled up and over an obstruction in the middle of the river and flipped Nathan over the top, allowing him to draw in a deep breath laced with muddy spray that caused him to gag and nearly go under again. Nathan flailed his arms out and managed to stay afloat long enough to grab another, cleaner, breath before something yanked on his foot, and he was pulled under again. Whatever had grabbed him, it was not letting go.

Nathan realized that he had stopped moving along with the river. It was rushing by him, stretching him out as he found himself locked in the grip of a submerged tree limb, his right foot wedged into the fork of one of its branches. The powerful current kept him from reaching back to twist his foot out of the fork, but he found that he could wiggle his foot inside his shoe. He thought if he could twist and flex his foot enough, he might be able to pull out of the shoe and be free of the branch. Nathan tried to pull up on his heel and twist his body at the same time, a task easy to accomplish on dry land but seemingly impossible as tons of water poured over him. After what seemed like an eternity, he felt his foot pop clear and, leaving his shoe behind, he bobbed to the surface once again.

As the river widened and the current slowed, it became easier for Nathan to stay on the surface. He really was not able to swim in a particular direction since the currents still had control of the situation, but at least his opportunities for breathing became more frequent and reliable. He also became aware of voices directing a search operation to find him. Nathan could not tell exactly from where the voices originated, but he was pretty sure they were back towards the bridge since the current was faster than anyone could move on land. Even if there was a search party along the shore, he certainly wasn't going to call attention to himself since they were likely to be Teshima's security guards. As he was swept along, Nathan began to feel like the river, even though it had tried to kill him, was now his friend.

However, some friendships were never intended to last long, and this was one of them. After Nathan went under the Puueo Bridge, he began to realize that he was reaching the edge of the dome. He had no idea what to expect when he reached that point, and he did not intend to find out. Nathan tried to swim gradually to his left, away from the town and toward the Ohai path that would lead back to Akina Park. He hoped that he could hide there for a while and that his disappearance would lead the guards to suspect that he had drowned and that they would give up the search. It was then that he thought of his parents and how devastated they would be if they, too, thought he had drowned. The sadness nearly made him stop swimming, but he quickly realized that if he did stop, his parents really would have something to mourn. Nathan picked up his pace.

Unfortunately for Nathan, picking up his pace was not enough to overcome the force of the river. The current hit a slight bend, picked up speed, and sent Nathan back towards the center. All the while, it continued to speed him closer to the dome's edge. Nathan's heart raced as he realized he was about to be carried out of Hilo Dome. He tried not to panic as the dome's edge loomed ever closer, but he was overwhelmed with fear when he noticed that the river was not flowing smoothly under the wall. He could see now that there was a foaming turbulence as the water hit the dome's edge and was drawn under in a series of whirlpools. Something was partially blocking the flow underwater.

Nathan turned away from the wall and made one last attempt to swim away from the dome's edge, but it was too little, too late. He grabbed one last breath as the whirlpools twisted him around and drew him under. He figured he could hold his breath until he emerged on the other side, a thought he firmly counted on until he was thrown hard against what felt like a series of metal poles in the water directly under the edge of the dome. The water pressed him firmly against the bars, and he could feel by the pressure on his body that they were spaced about one foot apart, too narrow to squeeze through. Not that it mattered. Nathan was pinned so tightly that he could not move to squeeze through, anyway. It felt like the dome had closed its mouth, and he was being clenched in its teeth.

Nathan managed to bend his knees enough to draw his feet closer to his body and plant them firmly against two of the bars. If he could just push his legs hard enough, he might be able to get his head up above the surface along the wall of the dome. With all the strength he had left, Nathan pushed against the bars, but instead of propelling him to the surface, the corroded ancient bars gave way, and Nathan shot through the gap as the river accelerated through the opening. When he struggled to the surface, Nathan was looking at the outside of Hilo Dome.

6
Outside Looking In

Nightfall came early and swiftly on the windward side of the island, the setting sun casting deep shadows on the bay as it slid behind Mauna Loa and Mauna Kea, the two mountains that make up the majority of the Big Island's mass. Nathan had never seen an unobstructed sunset before, and he was amazed at how beautiful the clouds looked as they changed colors through the oranges, reds, and violets of reflected sunlight beaming behind the massive, volcanic mountains. Treading water, Nathan looked back to the town. He could see the glow of Hilo's lights through the dome's plastic composite shell that had been the "sky" all his life. He thought about his parents inside the dome and wondered what they must be thinking with him missing.

The bay became bathed in darkness, and even though the waters of Hilo Bay were calm, Nathan felt a need to get to shore quickly since he was exhausted from his journey down the river and his passage through the gauntlet at the edge of the dome. The river's current had propelled him quite a distance out into the bay, so he began to do a gentle breaststroke, taking an angle slightly away from the dome itself so that he would eventually come ashore about one hundred meters north of where the Wailuku River emerged from the dome. Every so often, he swung his legs down to see if he could touch the bottom, and after just two tries, he felt the soft sand with his shoeless right foot. Standing, he slogged through the water until he reached the narrow sandy beach that ringed the north side of the bay. A shiver ran through him as he stared into the dark expanse of dense forest that seemed ready to swallow him whole. Although he was terrified of what might be lurking in the shadows, he was too exhausted to do anything about it. Nathan took off his remaining shoe and stretched out on the sand to ponder what his next move should be.

***

Jonathan Ohana returned home after what seemed like a week at the *kāhala* submarine docks. It had actually been just one day, but that day had stretched from the darkness of morning to the dusk of evening. As he walked through the door, he was thinking that it was good that Nathan had not come to work with him after all; the day had been far too long to hold a fourteen-year-old boy's interest. He flicked the light switch by the door, surprised that it appeared that no one was home. Jonathan walked through the small living room to the kitchen where the action usually was this time of the evening. He was starving and disappointed that there were no delicious dinner odors drifting out from the kitchen.

It soon became evident to Jonathan that no one was home. The house was not big enough for even one person to get lost in, let alone two. He went back to the living room to see if Lora had left a note, and finding none, he went to the kitchen to check there. Nothing. Jonathan picked up the phone hanging on the wall by the fridge and placed a call to Lora's office, even though he found it hard to believe that his wife was still at work this late in the evening. It was possible, of course, that there had been an emergency with the air handlers or the water supply, forcing her to stay late. But, if that were the case, she probably would have sent Nathan home. Lora's voicemail answered for her, and Jonathan left a brief message in case she was still there but unable to pick up. Deciding to wait a bit to see if they showed up, he opened the fridge, poured himself a glass of *jaboticaba* wine, and went into the living room to read the *Hilo Tribune Herald*.

It only took Jonathan about fifteen minutes to go through the few pages that comprised the weekly paper. There simply was not that much going on in Hilo to justify a bigger edition, and he had heard that many of the stories that might actually be important were being censored. He picked up his half-finished wine and went back to the kitchen. *I could start dinner*, he thought, *but since I haven't a clue as to where Lora and Nathan are, I have no idea as to when it should be ready*. Instead of fixing dinner, he placed a call to the Hilo Dome security office. To his surprise, the voice that answered was none other than Howard Teshima.

"Hello, Chief Teshima. This is Jonathan Ohana, Lora's husband. I was wondering if there had been an emergency of some kind today since Lora's not home from work yet."

There was a long pause before Teshima answered. "Actually, I was just about to call you. There has, in fact, been an emergency today. I was going to see if you could come down to the office."

Jonathan's nerves were on edge as his mind raced through all the possibilities. "Is Lora okay? Why do I need to come down?"

"It turns out that we had an air handler breakdown at the edge of the dome near Coconut Island that could possibly affect the *kāhala* operations for a few days, and, uh, we'll need to get your opinion on what we can do to get things operational as soon as possible." Teshima was secretly proud of how quickly he fabricated the lie he fed to Ohana. "Lora's working on it right now, but we could certainly use your input."

"Okay, Chief, I'll be there in a few minutes." As Jonathan hung up the phone, he wondered why Lora hadn't left a message for him on the phone or called him at work. *Maybe it just happened*, he thought as he went out the door and got on his bike. In any case, something still did not feel quite right about this, but there was nothing he could do except head down to the office to check it out for himself. Jonathan certainly could not have known that he would soon be joining his wife in captivity.

***

Nathan awoke with a start. The tide had come in, and the waves lapping at his feet woke him from a deep sleep brought on by the exhaustion he felt from the ordeal of his escape. He sat up and looked around, confused by not knowing how long he had slept, and a little bit scared about being out in the open. The expanse of sky and the view across the bay to the horizon was very unsettling for him having grown up under the protective cover of the dome. Nathan also realized he was chilled to the bone. His clothes were still wet, and he had spent a lot of time in the water. Even though the water in Hawaii was warm compared to many places on Earth, it still had the capacity to suck the body heat out of him.

The moon was just above the horizon, large and bright. Nathan found it hard to believe what he had read in his history books. People had actually once walked upon the moon's surface? With no planes, a human on the surface of the moon was incredibly hard to fathom, let alone rockets that left the Earth behind. However, the moon provided more than a mind-boggling spectacle; Nathan discovered it also made it fairly easy to investigate his surroundings.

Nathan stood up slowly. His muscles and joints ached from sleeping on the packed sand surface of the beach. He started walking towards the dense vegetation that encroached on the edge, but then stopped. The forest seemed alive with the sounds of insects and amphibians, especially the *coqui* frogs. It was much louder than inside the dome, probably because there were more of them. As he started walking again, he wondered how he had managed to fall asleep with the animal chorus emanating from the forest.

When he reached the vegetation, he turned and started to walk parallel to the edge of the forest, away from the dome. He was not sure if he could be seen from inside the dome during daylight hours, and he did not want to be detected until he had a plan for getting back inside. The plants were dense and seemed impenetrable, and the more he walked, the more discouraged he became about finding entry for concealment.

After what he estimated to be thirty or forty minutes, Nathan came to a point that jutted out into the bay. When he looked back towards the dome, he realized his path had formed a large crescent, and he was looking across an expanse of water at the glowing structure. To the left of the dome, he could make out the silhouette of Coconut Island, the place where his father worked. He continued on around the point, and for the first time was out of sight of the only place he had ever been in his life.

Nathan felt safer now in terms of being discovered by people from the dome, but he was beginning to get a creepy feeling about what might be in the forest. The moon was much higher now, casting long shadows from the trees and vines. The breeze coming off the water set the shadows in motion, animating the sounds broadcast from the deep shadows under the ferns and cycads. Several times, Nathan was certain he saw things scurrying under the fronds, but he never got a clear look at them to see exactly what they might be. And once, just once, he swore he saw a pair of radiant eyes staring back at him from the darkness. He picked up a large chunk of lava rock to use as a weapon in case the eyes came out of the forest. It was not much, but a false sense of security was better than none at all. The plan Nathan had formulated as he was walking was to find a clearing in the vegetation, find some fern fronds that he could gather up as bedding, and then get some rest until daylight. Now, he was not sure he could pull that off.

Finally, Nathan saw a break ahead in the dense vegetation. As he got closer, he realized the opening was the mouth of a fairly wide stream that spilled out of the forest and cut a path through the beach to the ocean. When he got to the stream, he looked to his right and could see that the waves were much higher now. He was no longer at the edge of Hilo Bay; he was looking at the open ocean. Turning back to the stream, he could make out what appeared to be a distinct path along the left side. A little warmer and drier from the walk, Nathan was tempted to spend the night on the beach, but he felt too exposed. His only choice, then, was to follow the path inland.

After just a few steps, it became difficult for Nathan to see the path clearly. The bright moonlight was not penetrating the dense foliage, and he stumbled frequently as vines reached out to grab his foot, or stones emerged from the soft dirt to stub his toes. At one point, the path veered close to the stream, and his right foot slipped off a rock and into the water with a loud splash that made him freeze in his tracks. It also silenced all the creatures in the immediate vicinity. Nathan listened for a moment, and as the *coqui* frogs resumed their chorus, he figured it was safe to move on.

Even with uncertain footing, moving along the trail was not terribly difficult; it was just slow going. After twenty or thirty meters, the path actually seemed to widen a bit, at which point Nathan began to wonder where the trail was leading. However, the thought that bothered him more than that was who or what had made the trail? He knew how unused areas of the dome could become overgrown, like Akina Park, and he figured vegetation out here would reclaim territory a lot more quickly. Something, or someone, had created and maintained this.

After ten more meters, the path opened into a clearing. The light was brighter here since the moon had climbed higher in the sky, and there were no trees to block it from illuminating the ground. To Nathan, it looked as though the vegetation in the clearing had been pressed to the ground. Whether it was accidental or intentional, he could not determine, but it made him hesitate about using an area like this to catch up on his sleep. What if whatever, or whomever, did this came back? However, he did not have any other options available, and there were plenty of soft ferns to gather up and pile near the edge of the clearing for a makeshift bed. Nathan decided it would have to do, at least for this first night. After fifteen minutes of collecting and arranging the fronds, he curled up and closed his eyes. At first, he thought about his parents and about what he needed to do in the morning, but not even the chorus of *coqui* frogs could prevent him from quickly slipping into a dreamless state of unconsciousness.

7
Ferals

The sun was peeking above the treetops when Nathan opened his eyes. Startled, he found himself looking directly into the face of the smallest, scruffiest cat he had ever seen. Not that he had seen many; few people kept pets in Hilo Dome, and if they did, they were usually birds or rodents. Seeing Nathan stir, the cat took two steps away, arched its back, turned sideways, and let out a very convincing hiss as it puffed out what little fur it had. Its tail looked like a worn-out bottlebrush. Nathan could not help but laugh seeing this tiny animal put on such a courageous display, but as he sat up to get a better look, the cat crab-walked sideways, then turned tail and ran for the underbrush. He thought that if the cat was as dangerous as things got on the outside, then he did not have a lot to worry about. It certainly was not one of the radioactive monsters featured in the Hilo Dome rumor mill.

If there were monsters, they would have to wait. Finding food and water was now Nathan's top priority. He was extremely thirsty, and his stomach growled, not having been fed since breakfast the previous day. Eggs would be just fine now, and he really wished he could find an L & L Drive In out here. Nathan decided that he would have to take his chances by drinking from the stream, even though his mother had frequently described a variety of aquatic life forms that could cause severe intestinal ailments if the water was not treated. He made his way over to the stream, knelt down, and scooped out some water in his cupped hands. It tasted clean and sweet, fresher than dome water. After drinking a bit more, Nathan turned his attention to finding food.

Gathering food to eat was not something Nathan had ever done before. Everything he had eaten in the dome had come from shops or from the farmers' market on Mamo Street. He began to walk around the clearing to see if he could locate some trees bearing fruit or nuts that he might recognize as being edible. He was much more concerned about eating something poisonous than he was about being infected by some invisible bug in the water.

After walking almost the entire way around the clearing, he was beginning to give up hope of finding anything at all, let alone something recognizable as food. Finally, he spotted something familiar, something that he had for breakfast several times a week. A small papaya tree was set back from the clearing, and it was loaded with fruit. Nathan was able to find several ripe ones easily within his reach. After he picked one, he tackled the problem of getting to the flesh inside.

He was already salivating when he found a dry-looking branch that had probably been on the ground for a while, not far from the tree. When Nathan bent it, it snapped with a sharp crack, leaving a slanted break on one side that ended in a sharp point. It was crude, but it would certainly work well enough to split the fruit open. After making several jagged cuts, he managed to open the papaya. He quickly scooped out the numerous seeds from its center and carved out the soft, sweet flesh with his makeshift knife. Papaya had never tasted so good!

After finishing his second papaya, Nathan felt better. His clothes had dried, and he had found water and food. He figured it was time to make his way back towards the beach. He wanted to get back to the point he had rounded the night before to get a look at the dome in the daylight. Having never been on the outside, Nathan had no idea what the dome actually looked like. He was hoping some reconnoitering would suggest some ideas about getting back inside without too much trouble or being detected by the security force. He was guessing that they had given up the search by this point, and although it would crush his parents, it was better that everyone thought he was dead, lost to the waters of the Wailuku.

He found the entrance to the path he had followed the previous night and started back. He was making good progress, much better than he did in the dark, when he heard a loud grunting sound. Nathan froze in his tracks. He had never heard anything like that before, and it seemed to be somewhere ahead of him on the path. The path took a curve to the right about ten meters in front of him to follow the course of the stream, so he was not sure exactly how far ahead it might be. However, in addition to the grunting, it was obvious that it was ripping through a lot of vegetation. It almost sounded as though it was uprooting small trees. Given all the noise, Nathan figured it had to be big. Real big.

The grunting and shredding noise seemed to be getting farther away, and then it stopped entirely. He thought he could detect the rustling sound of something heavy moving away through the vegetation, very different from the ripping sound he had heard previously. Even so, Nathan could not make his feet move either forwards or backwards down the path. Finally, after several moments of silence, the birds began to sing once again, and everything seemed to return to normal. Nathan did not know how long he had been holding his breath, but it was finally released as he let out a big sigh of relief. He thought it would be best if he returned to the clearing to give whatever it was time to move out of the area, so he turned and retraced his steps.

As Nathan broke into the clearing, he was distressed to hear the grunting sound again, but it was not coming from behind him on the path. It was directly across the clearing, coming from a dense stand of *hāpu'u* ferns. Once again, he froze, and the noise stopped, just as it did on the path. Beads of sweat formed on his forehead, and he looked cautiously from side to side to see if there was a place to hide. There were some small *hala* and mesquite trees close by to his right; he thought about climbing one, but none of them seemed strong enough to support his weight. However, getting deeper into the wooded area behind them might be just enough to conceal him if he crouched down behind the spreading support roots of the *hala*.

Just as Nathan took his first step, his escape plans became irrelevant. A huge wild boar burst into the clearing. It pawed the ground with its right front foot, and snorting, looked directly at him. There was no hiding at this point from a beast that, at the shoulders, stood as tall as Nathan, and weighed at least seven hundred pounds. The boar's curved tusks protruded ten inches out of its mouth, and the brown bristles on his back stood out like a badly cut Mohawk. The pictures Nathan had seen of Hawaiian *pua'a* certainly did not depict an animal of this size, and as it lowered its head to charge, Nathan overcame his fear and made a break for the *hala* and mesquite.

The boar was quick, much quicker than expected for its size. Nathan knew it would either gore or trample him before he reached the trees, but there was nothing to do but to keep running. The boar had closed to within ten meters when suddenly the word "DUCK" erupted in his head. It was so forceful that he dove straight for the ground, and as he did, he felt something whiz by his ear so close he thought it may have clipped his hair. The boar squealed in pain but did not stop his charge. Nathan rolled over twice and got to his hands and knees, ready to sprint for cover. A quick look at the enraged *pua'a* revealed the cause of its distress; an arrow was sticking directly out of his forehead.

An arrow?

Nathan was so shocked at the sight that he momentarily forgot about running, and as he stared at the beast, a second arrow abruptly pierced the pig's right eye. The boar squealed and spun around to his right as if he could still see in that direction. Spinning in circles like a porcine tornado, his momentum carried him towards where Nathan continued to crouch. Just when Nathan thought the *pua'a* would spin right over him, the pig stopped, shook his head as if trying to rid himself of the offending arrows, and fell over. He was so close Nathan could feel the boar's hot breath as it shuddered and gave one last sigh as it expired. Trembling, Nathan got slowly to his feet and stood over the dead animal.

That was close! Nathan spun around as the words formed in his head, and for a moment, he thought he was looking at an odd reflection of himself.

At the edge of the clearing in the entrance to the path he had just traveled stood a young girl with sandy blonde hair and green eyes. Her long hair was pulled straight back and woven into a braid intertwined with thin cords made of *hala* leaves. The color of her hair contrasted sharply with dark skin that matched the browns in her *kapa* cloth *pa'u* wrap-around. Slung over her shoulder was a quiver, also of *kapa*, that contained the arrows for the longbow in her left hand. She took several steps into the clearing, her eyes fixed on Nathan.

"Who are you? Where did you come from?" Her lips did not move, but the words filled Nathan's brain nonetheless.

Nathan did not know how to answer. He had nothing to write with, so he tried to describe with hand and arm motions the direction from which he had come and what the shape of the dome was like. As he did this, he thought about the words he would have used if he could write it down.

"So, you claim to be from the enclosure. Considering how you are dressed, that might just be possible." Again, her lips did not move, yet he understood. "You didn't say your name."

He was thinking, *"How can I tell her my name's Nathan Ohana when I can't...?"*

"Your last name is 'family?'"

Ohana. Somehow, she knew I was thinking about my name. He looked directly at her and thought, "Yes, Ohana; it means 'family,' but it's also my last name: Nathan Ohana."

She walked over to him. Standing so close, Nathan could see she was just as tall as he was, and very muscular. "Well, Nathan Ohana, I think you need to follow me back to my village. We need to tell my *ohana* about this *pua'a* so it can be butchered and brought back for food." She turned as if to leave, and then looked back over her shoulder. "And you will need to explain how you got here and why you are outside the enclosure, if that is, in fact, where you really come from." She paused, and then smiled slightly. "What's the matter? Has it developed *pukas* through which people can crawl now? Follow me." She started walking toward the path, not even checking to see if he was behind her. Nathan blushed slightly. She seemed so confident, and having just been rescued by her, he felt like a total klutz. *I guess I better thank her for saving me*, he thought.

"You're welcome," her voice spoke in his head.

Nathan was confused. This interaction he was having was different from what he experienced inside the dome. Nathan had always known that he could "hear" actual conversations and the thoughts of other people in his head. That was how his mother had warned him back at her office. He also knew that he was never able to communicate with anyone else in the dome simply by thinking what he wanted them to know. Having this girl be able to read his mind would take some getting used to. He caught up with her and fell in step behind, trying to keep his mind blank.

She moved quickly along the path, and in about one quarter of the time it took Nathan to negotiate the distance the night before, they emerged on the beach and into the bright sunlight. She stopped, looked towards the point as if considering it as a possible destination, then turned and headed in the opposite direction. Nathan ran a few steps to catch up, and now walked along beside her.

Giving his new "voice" a try, he thought, "That really was incredible shooting back there. Thanks, again, for saving me."

No reply.

"You know, to thank you properly, I really should know your name. After all, you know mine. I mean, even Ferals have to have names."

He stopped and shook his head. "Ferals!" That thought in particular was not intended for her. "Real smooth," he thought, but not just to himself. She stopped, turned, and took a step back toward him so that she was standing no more than a foot away.

"You're right, Mr. Ohana; it wasn't 'real smooth.' Ferals? Is that what we are called? It somehow doesn't sound particularly flattering. However, my name is

Kayli Pahinui, and my shooting was just okay, as far as I'm concerned. I was hoping to down the *pua'a* with just one arrow." She smiled and poked her finger in his chest. "When you 'thalk,' you don't know how to separate your 'voice' from your thoughts, do you? It certainly will be interesting to know what you are thinking about me."

This time, Nathan really was embarrassed. His mind raced. "Thinking about her? Why would I be thinking about her? I mean, yeah, she saved me from the pig, and she's ..." He stopped. "I guess that all came through, too." She nodded. "So, if you can control this communication, this 'thalk,' I guess I better learn how to separate my private thoughts from my conversational thoughts, if that's possible."

Kayli smiled. "Oh, it's possible, and it would be very wise to learn. Think-talk, or thalk, is a very important skill to master when you are around your enemy," she hesitated, "or one you love." She started off down the beach. Love? Nathan shook his head and decided to pursue the other line of thought. He had to run a few steps to catch up.

"You have enemies?"

She looked at Nathan suspiciously. "Yes. In fact, how do I know you are not an enemy?" She looked down at Nathan's feet. "Of course, I doubt that an enemy would be found walking around unarmed, in his socks, wearing a purple shirt, and under attack by a pig."

Nathan realized that Kayli was in her bare feet, while he was still slogging around in his now tattered and dirty socks. What was that saying about first impressions? He quickly leaned over and pulled his socks off and stuffed them in his pockets.

"Saving them for something?"

"No, uh, I, um, just didn't want to litter the beach." After they walked a bit, he tried again. "So, about the 'enemies' thing ..."

"Yes, we do have some possible enemies. For example, our ancestors were not treated well by the people who built the dome, and then they excluded us from its protection. That has not been forgotten." Kayli paused and looked at Nathan. "Or forgiven. While the dome inhabitants do not seem hostile, we do not really trust them." She paused. "Sorry."

Nathan said, "No, don't be sorry. That's understandable."

Kayli went on. "We have also had encounters with people from Kona side, not recently, but within the last twenty years. We have an abundance of fresh water and food while they seem to have little and are restricted to an area we simply know as 'Cook.' We believe they used to have more, but we are pretty certain a large volcanic eruption and lava flow destroyed most of their fertile areas. They apparently were considering an attack to expand and take over our village and resources. A small, armed reconnaissance patrol from their area was discovered by one of our hunting groups and a fight broke out. The hunting group summoned people from my village and a series of running skirmishes occurred in the forest all around the village. In the end, everyone in their patrol was killed, so the people back in Cook probably never really figured out what happened to them. We also lost several people."

Nathan was stunned. There seemed to be a lot going on outside the dome, that calm, restricted enclosure that had basically been the whole world to him up until about twenty-four hours ago. He felt bad about the way Kayli's people had been treated. Why were they excluded? Who made those decisions? The answers certainly were not in the history books he read inside the dome. And people from the other side of the island? If the Cook people thought Kayli's people had resources, what did they think of Hilo Dome? Kayli let him dwell on these thoughts as they continued up the beach.

Nathan's thoughts dissipated when Kayli's voice said, "We're here."

Nathan could see a broad stream, larger than the one he followed the previous night, spilling out across the beach and into the ocean. As he followed it up-stream, he could see that it poured over huge blocks of concrete. Rusted metal bars projected out from many of them, making the blocks appear like huge stone insects that had drowned in the stream. He was having trouble trying to figure out what they were when Kayli explained. "That used to be the great bridge. It towered high over the stream, or so I've been told, until about thirty years ago when a huge storm caused the water to erode the base away, sending the entire structure down into the valley. That bridge used to connect the two sides of our village, and eight people died when it went down. Most of the people from the south side then relocated to the north since it was already the biggest part. My village is Honoli'i, named after the stream."

Nathan and Kayli walked through cool fresh water that came up to their knees, and then started climbing uphill along a path beside the stream. The climb was fairly steep and soon turned away from the stream to the north. At the top of what seemed like a wide plateau, they turned inland again until they came to a worn, paved path. The asphalt had split in many places, giving way to victorious grasses and small ferns, but there was a very clear track leading to the north once more. After five minutes, Nathan could see that the heavy vegetation on either side of him ended just ahead.

As they emerged from the wooded area, Nathan could see a sprawling village, a hodge-podge of dilapidated houses, old stores, and traditional-looking thatched huts that seemed to be in much better shape than the houses and store fronts. The asphalt path they had followed carved a straight line down the middle and was obviously the center of most of the activity in the village. People of all ages, both men and women, moved quickly back and forth across the path, going about their daily business and oblivious to Kayli and Nathan as they stood at the edge of the town. Nathan also noted that all of them, to one degree or another, looked a lot like him.

Kayli let Nathan absorb all of this for a few moments, and then said, "Come on, I need to tell Edward Park, one of our village butchers, about the *pua'a*. He'll get some men to butcher the pig to bring it back here. My family will get some, as a reward for my hunting prowess," Kayli smiled at this, "and then he will sell the rest in his shop. After we see him, it will be time for you to meet with my father."

Nathan was nervous. "With your father? Why your father?"

Kayli smiled. "Because he's the village leader here in Honoli'i, and he'll be the one who convenes the village elders to decide what to do with you."

"What to do with me?" Nathan did not particularly like the tone of that, but there was nothing he could do at this point. Resigned to his fate, he walked with Kayli into the village.

8
Honoli'i

Chief Teshima met Jonathan Ohana at the front door when he arrived at the office. "Hello, Jonathan. I'm glad you could come over on short notice. I'm hoping we can figure out a way to divert some of the air from other handlers to your part of the dome in case we have to totally shut down the one near the submarine operations. We're not sure how healthy conditions will be for your workers if we can't." Without waiting for a response, he turned and started down the hallway, talking as he went. "I'm hoping that you and Lora will be able to come up with some solutions to help minimize any interruptions to our fishing schedule." Jonathan followed without comment, but he found Teshima's comments to be suspicious since the sub base air handlers operated on their own using the solar panels as their source of electricity.

Teshima stopped in front of a door, flipped two latches, and said, "We'll all meet in here. Why don't you go in and wait with Lora while I go get the mayor. He wants to be in on this discussion." He opened the door, and as soon as Jonathan entered the room, Teshima closed the door and locked it once again. The chief of security then went to find Mayor Hapuna, not to bring him to a meeting, but to tell him that Jonathan was now an honored guest along with his wife.

Jonathan turned back towards the door as he heard the locks click behind him, and then he quickly looked back at his wife. Her head was in her hands, and when she looked up, he could see that she was obviously distraught, her eyes red and swollen from crying. When she realized Jonathan was locked in with her, she jumped from her chair and threw her arms around him.

After a short time, she backed away from him and said, "It's Nathan. They chased him; the security guards chased him on orders from Hapuna and Teshima because they thought he uncovered something that the two of them were planning that would really upset the people of Hilo. Nathan got away, but then they eventually cornered him on the bridge over the Wailuku." She stopped, and Jonathan came over and put his arm around her as he sat beside her.

"Jonathan, Nathan jumped. He jumped, and they never found him."

Jonathan could not believe what he was hearing. What could Nathan know that would be so important? Why would Teshima and Hapuna be afraid of what a teenage boy might or might not know? He tried to think about what the Wailuku must be like given the recent rains, and as he did, a sense of dread filled him. Nathan knew how to swim; Jonathan had taught him at the Waiākea Pond near their home. But the river was now swollen and extremely treacherous. He knew he had to give Lora something positive to cling to even if he really did not believe it himself.

"Nathan will be okay. He's a good swimmer, and he's probably clever enough to elude the guards over in that area. Don't forget, that's where he used to play all the time when he was younger. He knows it inside and out."

Lora looked at her husband. "You really think so? I mean, you may be right, but what do we do now? How do we get him back? What's going to happen to us now that we know something is seriously wrong here in the mayor's office?"

Jonathan knew his wife was asking some serious questions, questions that he could not answer at the moment. He just hoped that Nathan was safe. Somewhere.

**

It had taken only a few minutes to arrive at the front of Kayli's *hale noho* after leaving Edward Park's butcher shop, and Nathan's purple shirt had drawn only a few stares as they made their way through the village. Almost all the clothing worn by the people of the village was either made of printed *kapa* or some other light tan material that had not been decorated with the traditional ornate printing. Everyone seemed to be too busy going about their daily business to pay much attention to him, but he paid attention to them. No one spoke directly to anyone; thalk was the currency of conversation.

The Pahinui *hale*, located on the far side of the village and several blocks off the main path, was a combination of the remnants of an ancient, small ranch house and a thatched extension that more than doubled the area of the original building. The *pili* grass roof was supported by sturdy, hardwood beams and supports, lashed together with thick braided rope. Nathan was impressed by the overall size of the structure. It was at least fifty percent larger than his house in the dome. In fact, most of the places he saw were built in a similar fashion and were quite large.

Kayli told Nathan to wait outside while she went in to get her father. Nathan's stomach was doing flip-flops since he had no idea how Kayli's father would view his arrival in their world. Kayli had said the people of Hilo Dome had not been forgiven for excluding them when the enclosure was constructed. And even though that exclusion had occurred long before Nathan was born, he was still a member of the dome community. Nathan wondered what forms of punishment or jail the Ferals had. He also made a note to himself to stop thinking of them as "Ferals." In fact, he was not sure what they called themselves. Nathan was beginning to wonder what was taking Kayli so long when his thoughts were interrupted by the appearance of her father in the entranceway.

Sam Pahinui was tall and slender, well over six feet tall, a full head taller than Nathan. As with the other people of Honoliʻi, his bright green eyes, bronze skin, and sandy blond hair created a handsome study in contrasts. It was obvious to Nathan from Mr. Pahinui's posture that he commanded respect from those around him. His imposing figure made him even more nervous, but this feeling was quickly dispelled when Sam Pahinui extended his hand and smiled.

"Welcome to Honoliʻi."

Nathan smiled, shook his hand, and thought back, "Thank you, and thanks to Kayli. I suppose she told you how she saved me."

"Yes, she did. You should be glad she was out on one of her favorite pastimes—hunting. She wasn't expecting to bring down one of the largest *puaʻa* we've ever seen." He looked over at her with a smile. "Or so she says."

He turned back to Nathan. "And she certainly wasn't expecting to bring someone home with her, in particular, a resident of the enclosure." Sam Pahinui paused for a moment, studying Nathan. "She also told me you know how to think-talk. It's obvious now that you can do this quite well. Given that, I'd like to learn more about you, and the enclosure, before I convene the elders. Please, come in."

Nathan followed Sam Pahinui into his home. The large room they entered was sparsely furnished, but there were a number of woven mats on the floor. Kayli and her father each sat down on one and motioned for Nathan to sit on a mat facing them. As he sat down, Nathan took in the *kapa* wall hangings that decorated all the walls. They made the room seem very comfortable, even without furniture. He felt more at ease about talking with Kayli and her father now, even though his immediate future remained uncertain.

Sam began their conversation. "So, why don't you tell us how you got here and why you are outside the dome."

Nathan began to tell his story slowly, not sure how much he should share with Sam and Kayli. But as he went on, he felt more certain that these people had no intention of harming him, so he went into more and more detail. He told them all he knew about conditions in the dome and about the conversations he intercepted between the mayor and his chief of security. He described his harrowing escape from the government office building, his subsequent trip down the Wailuku River, and finally his exit from the dome.

Throughout the story, Sam Pahinui watched Nathan intently, as if trying to discern whether he was telling the truth or not. Only when Nathan described the plan to "neutralize" the Ferals and take their resources did his look become somber, and he let out a deep sigh.

"What you have told us is very troubling, but not terribly surprising. We have been anticipating for some time an opening of the dome, but we were not sure what the relationship would be like between the people of our town and the dome inhabitants." Sam paused for a moment, still looking at Nathan. "Tell me more about your family. For instance, what are your parents like?"

Nathan described his mother and father, how they looked and what they did for a living. He became very sad as he recalled them, and at times he had to stop for a moment to allow his emotions to settle enough so that he could continue to thalk. Sam Pahinui glanced at Kayli frequently during Nathan's recollections, trying to imagine what Nathan's parents must be going through.

"So, both your parents hold positions within the dome government, but neither was aware of the plans to open the dome or, as you say, 'neutralize' those of us outside the dome."

"That's right. They wouldn't have been involved in anything like that, and I don't think the majority of the people who live in the dome would want it either."

"So, you think maybe Teshima and Hapuna want to solidify their positions at the head of the government and extend the range of their powers by taking over our community?"

"That would be my guess. I think they like being in control."

"You said your father is in charge of the *kāhala* farming operation for the dome. How long has he been doing that?"

"Since before I was born. I'm not sure exactly how long."

Sam Pahinui thought about this for several minutes before continuing, as if it were important in some way. "What are the people like who live in the dome? Are there any who look like you or who can thalk?"

That was an odd jump in the conversation, Nathan thought to himself. Before he could respond, Sam Pahinui explained. "The reason I ask is that we are pretty sure our ability to thalk is a genetic mutation, a trait that came about after the island received a low dose of radiation after the war. We're not sure how those inside the dome were affected by that."

"As far as I know, I'm the only one who can think-talk."

"Does anyone else look like you?"

"Um, no."

"So, you've never thought about how different you were."

Nathan did not know what to say. He certainly had thought about it. His inability to fit in had kept him awake at night and had made him miserable at times. Now, with all he had seen in Honoli'i, he realized there were many more people just like him. He was not a freak, and he was not alone. Nathan just didn't know how to explain all this to the two kind people who had rescued him and seemed ready to provide him with shelter. He looked up at Sam Pahinui, and realized he already had.

9
Spies

From a small outcropping of lava rock that overlooked Honoli'i, Abe Hasegawa and Michael Wai watched as Nathan entered Sam Pahinui's *hale*. They had been observing the Hilo Dome for several days when they picked up Nathan's trail, totally by chance, after they saw him appear on the beach just outside the dome on Hilo Bay. They had been sent from Cook to find out what conditions were like in and around the dome, looking for any signs of weakness in preparation for a possible attack. Abe and Michael were well aware that, twenty years ago, a larger and well-armed contingent from Cook had been sent on a similar mission and were never heard from again. This time, Cook decided to try a more stealthy and subtle approach, using pairs of spies to spread out over a wider area of the Big Island to gather information, hopefully without engaging any of the locals.

Abe and Michael had followed Nathan as he made his way off the beach and into the forest. They had debated whether or not they should capture Nathan as he made his way along the trail. Michael wanted to question the boy, insisting that they could extract invaluable information from him, but Abe was afraid that suspicions would be raised if the kid failed to return home, since after questioning he would have to be eliminated. They had no idea that Nathan was actually escaping from trouble inside the dome, and he had no real expectation, at that point, of whether or not he would ever return. The argument was settled when Kayli appeared and saved Nathan from the giant *pua'a*. Even though skilled in the art of *lua*, an ancient Hawaiian bone-breaking fighting technique, after seeing her skill with a bow they decided to follow them from a safe distance to see where the two teens would go.

Michael and Abe had not yet seen Honoli'i, but when they finally did after following Kayli and Nathan, they were very impressed by the number of people, quality of housing, and evidence of a thriving society. They were also more than a little curious about how all the people looked. Blond hair? No one they knew had blond hair. They were not close enough to realize that this physical attribute was not the only characteristic that set the people of Honoli'i apart from all the others who lived on the Big Island, or anywhere else that they knew of, for that matter.

More than anything, Michael and Abe were excited about the vast acres of crops, trees, and livestock they witnessed. Rice, taro, fruit and macadamia nut trees, and pens filled with goats and pigs were laid out before them like a *luau* waiting to happen. Fenced fields on the edge of the village were home to well over a hundred head of cattle, more than they had ever seen in one place.

Conditions in Cook had not been good for many decades after large areas of orchards and other agricultural areas had been buried beneath a meter or two of lava. Fruit and macadamia nut trees could not take root in the cooled lava rock, and even if they could, they would take years to reach maturity. The *'ōhi'a lehua* trees did just fine, but people cannot live very long eating pretty flowers. The lava substrate was also devoid of the fertile soil that supported the crops that once grew on the formerly lush mountainside above Kailua Kona and the lands south of Kealakeakua Bay. With little rain and no vegetation or soil to hold the little that did fall, the people of Cook had to look elsewhere, or die.

Led by the aggressive ruler Alfred Kawananakoa, who, with visions of grandeur, had assumed the title Kamehameha VI, the people of Cook waged war with their neighbors in the sparsely populated land to the south and east, easily taking relatively productive areas that were once open to grazing and planted with macadamia trees. However, virtually all the cattle had been eaten shortly after the nuclear devastation centuries ago, and very little had been done since that time to repopulate the herds. Pigs and goats, no longer in pens, ran wild and had to be hunted down. The people had reverted to a modified hunter-gatherer way of existence. The biggest problem was that the water supply was inconsistent; short, torrential downpours were followed by extensive periods of drought. Kawananakoa, as the modern Kamehameha, decided that it was time to expand his modest empire into fertile Hilo. Judging by the way the winds blew across the island, he suspected that there was plenty of rainfall on the windward side. Scouts, like Michael and Abe, were assigned the task of finding out just how rich and how vulnerable Hilo and villages such as Honoli'i might be.

Michael and Abe decided to watch Honoli'i for a few more days and then return to Hilo to complete their assessment of the dome's vulnerability. Kawananakoa had predicted that any towns along the coast could be attacked successfully from elevated positions originating on the mountainside below Kilauea

Crater with a simultaneous assault from the water. They were excited by the fact that everything they had seen so far seemed to indicate that this would be a strategy worth pursuing, especially if they could discover a way to penetrate the dome. In any case, Honoli'i looked extremely valuable and possibly vulnerable.

***

Unaware of the spies assessing the village, Kayli and Sam Pahinui continued their conversation with Nathan. Several times, Sam returned to the topic of how people looked and acted in the dome, and also how Nathan's father, Jonathan, ran the *kāhala* operation. Finally, Nathan asked, "Why are you so curious about the *kāhala*? Do you have anything like that here in Honoli'i?"

Sam smiled. "Actually, we don't. We have something like it in Hilo Bay." He could see Nathan was confused by the response. "You see, we've been, shall we say, 'sampling' your father's product for a number of years now. We knew the fish were being tended to and harvested by boats that arrived underwater. We saw all this from our *wa'a kaukahi*."

Nathan looked confused. "Wait. From your what?"

"Oh. Sorry. That's the Hawaiian word for our canoes," Sam explained. "After a while, we realized the submarines, and therefore the people in the dome, could not sense our presence, so we kept closer tabs on the schedule for the release of young fish into the pens, feeding, and finally, the harvest. When we knew the underwater boats would not be in service, we made plans for our people to be there, on the surface in our canoes, with our own hand nets and lines. It was, as I believe the old expression went, 'like shooting fish in a barrel.'"

Nathan was stunned. He could not believe people were actually raiding his father's pens. He knew his father would sometimes complain that a harvest was less than usual, but Jonathan always attributed the low numbers to disease or possible holes in the pen netting, not human intervention.

"I'm sorry if it caused your father any trouble or worry," Sam added. "We also knew that the entire pen would be taken back through a cave to port for a total harvest, and probably some repairs. We really had to avoid the area during those times since our *wa'a kaukahi* could be caught up in the pens or struck by one of the subs and either capsized or dragged back to the port."

Nathan was curious. "Did that ever happen?"

Sam was silent for a long time before he answered. "Just once. A group of families were out fishing together. It was not unusual for an entire family to take part since the kids could help and learn the whole process. Net fishing, as we call it, was always considered a very safe activity when the bay was calm. However, this was the first time anyone had ever witnessed an entire pen being retrieved. One canoe was hit by a submarine, and it sheared off the outrigger, making the boat very unstable. It got caught up in the netting as the top was being cinched tight to prepare it for collection. As the net came close to being pulled into cave leading to the underwater port, the canoe capsized, spilling the couple who were desperately paddling to escape the net, out into the water." Sam paused.

Nathan hesitated, "I'm afraid to ask, but what happened to them?"

Sam sighed. "They tried to cling to the overturned hull, but it was too slick to grasp, especially with the sub pulling it along in the net. They slipped off and were washed out of the netting as it surged towards the entrance the cave. A second sub that was assisting in the net retrieval either struck them or they were pulled underwater by the turbulence of its propeller."

Sam paused once more. "We recovered their bodies after the subs disappeared into the cave."

Nathan was quite upset by this. Even though it was an accident, he did not want to think about his father's operation being responsible for people dying.

Sam sensed his distress, but there was more to the story. "Because the mother had been nursing, they had their baby along with them in what they thought was a safe place while they fished, tucked away in the bottom of the canoe, strapped in under the bow. This area of the boat was scalloped out and had some shade to protect the baby from the sun. When the canoe capsized and the top of the net closed over it, the baby was not found. The canoe was lost as it was pulled into the port with the fish in the net." Sam's eyes were visibly moist when he finished describing what had happened. Nathan did not know what to say. "Obviously, once they found the *waʻa kaukahi* in the net, people in the dome could form some definite conclusions about our existence."

Kayli reached out to touch Nathan's arm. "My father and mother were in the canoe nearest to them. The couple were my parents' best friends. My father still thinks there might have been something he could have done to prevent the tragedy." Kayli looked toward her father. "But there wasn't, was there, Father?"

Sam sighed again. "No. No, I guess there wasn't."

Sam stood up slowly and looked at his daughter. "Kayli, your mother should be home soon. I think she went to get some vegetables at the market. You can show Nathan to the guest room and maybe find a change of clothes for him. I'm sure there's something that doesn't fit your brothers anymore. I need to gather the elders together to discuss what I have learned from Nathan." He turned to Nathan. "As far as I am concerned, you are welcome to stay here as long as you like. I'm not sure all the elders will agree, but I can be very persuasive." He smiled at Nathan's worried look. "Don't worry; we'll work something out. You'll eat with our family tonight, okay?"

Hearing Sam's invitation to stay with them brought Nathan around from his thoughts concerning the capsized canoe. Nathan smiled hesitantly. "Sure, I'd like that, especially since I really don't want to go back into the forest to look for papaya now that I know what else is out there!"

As he left the room, Sam said, "Good. I'll see you both this evening."

***

Michael and Abe watched Sam leave his *hale* and head for the center of town. They tracked him until he entered an old building that had a lot of foot traffic, as though it was a meeting point of some kind. After about an hour, they decided to leave Honoli'i and return to Hilo to take a closer look at the dome structure itself. Unless some point of weakness could be found, the invasion of Hilo by Kamehameha VI would never happen. However, both Abe and Michael believed that Honoli'i would prove to be an easy conquest.

10
History Lesson

Just before the Pahinui family gathered for dinner, clouds rolled in off the ocean, and rain began to pour down. Nathan, wearing *kapa* shorts and a shirt Kayli found for him in her brother's room, heard the water striking the roof and walked out of the front entrance of the *hale*. Standing in the opening, he stared at the sky, inviting the rain to pelt him in the face. Even though the water was beginning to soak his newly acquired clothes, he could not tear himself away from the simple phenomenon of precipitation, something no one in the dome had ever experienced. So fascinated was he that he did not hear Kayli come up behind him.

"Nathan! You're getting soaked! What are you doing outside?"

Nathan, trancelike, turned as her thoughts entered his head. "It's just that I've never seen, or felt, anything like this," he explained as he turned back to look at the sky.

"Well, now that you're staying here with us, you'll have plenty of time to experience it since it rains here a lot!"

Nathan turned back to Kayli, took one last look at the swift moving clouds, and reluctantly came back inside the *hale*. "She's right," he thought a bit sadly as the memory of his parents washed over him just as the rain had done moments before. "I'll have plenty of time to experience many new things now that I'm outside the dome."

"Of course I'm right," Kayli added. "Now come on, everyone's gathering for dinner. It's lucky for us the rain held off as long as it did since most of the meal was cooked outside." Nathan realized that, once again, what he thought were his private thoughts had been projected out for everyone to intercept. "I'll never get used to this," he thought.

"Sure, you will."

Nathan sighed and followed Kayli into the dining area. Places for the Pahinui family were set in a circle on woven mats on the ground, a wooden dish and bowl marking each person's seat for the meal. Sam and Kayli's two older brothers, Byl and Aaron, were already seated, while Kayli's mother, Layla, and her Auntie Bernice shuttled back and forth from the kitchen bringing out bowls and plates of food that they placed in the center of the circle.

"Nathan, have a seat by me, and Kayli can sit beside you." Sam motioned to the empty spot beside him. "We're starting with *pupus,* and then we'll move on to the main course." The look on Nathan's face prompted Sam to add, "We usually don't eat this lavishly, but you are a special guest tonight. Don't look for this kind of spread in the future unless it's a special occasion."

Nathan looked a bit perplexed since he could not identify some of the things he saw spread out before him. Kayli realized this and began to describe some of the appetizers. "This is *tako poke,* very tasty octopus. This bowl is *kim chee.* If you like spicy food, this is for you. Don't mind the smell; it tastes great! And these bamboo skewers have pieces of grilled goat." Nathan looked at Kayli dubiously. She took Nathan's plate and spooned out some *poke, kim chee,* and added a skewer of the goat. "Go ahead, you'll love it!"

Layla and Bernice seated themselves, and everyone began to pass around the *pupus.* As they began to eat, they would occasionally glance over at Nathan to see how he was doing. Nathan noticed that Byl and Aaron were big eaters and dove right in, eating the goat right off the skewers and shoveling the *kim chee* and *poke* into their mouths with chopsticks.

Must be good, he thought to himself.

"It is!" came a chorus of thalk from everyone seated in the circle. Nathan laughed at himself for thinking "out loud" again and, picking up his chopsticks, attacked the *kim chee* just like Byl and Aaron.

"Hot! Hot!" Nathan looked up to see everyone staring at him. "But very good," he added swiftly. He could feel the spice climb up his throat to the back of his nose, and his eyes began to water, but he really did like the taste. He tried the *poke* next, and though it was a little chewy, he found it delicious, not as spicy as the *kim chee.* Finally, Nathan picked up the goat skewer. The only meat he ever had in the dome was chicken, so he was a little hesitant, but after tasting it, he finished it quickly and added another skewer to his plate. "Mrs. Pahinui, this is absolutely delicious!"

"Thanks, Nathan. I made the *poke* and *kim chee,* but the goat is Auntie Bernice's specialty."

Kayli added, "If you think this is good, wait until you see and taste the rest of the meal."

Kayli was right. After the *pupus*, Layla and Bernie brought in bowls of *kalua* pig, pork *lau lau*, *'uala* seasoned with *limu*, *poi*, and fresh pineapple. Nathan recognized *lau lau*, the delicious, steamed packet of fish and meat wrapped in *ti* leaves because he would occasionally get chicken *lau lau* at the L & L, but this was far better. And *'uala*, the purple sweet potato, was found in the dome, but never seasoned with seaweed and sea salt.

As everyone settled into their meals, Sam addressed Nathan's situation. "The elders agreed that you should stay with us in Honoli'i, at least for the near future. I told them that you would be our guest for as long as was needed. What troubled them the most, as it did me, was your description of how the attitude of the government in Hilo has changed, along with the deteriorating conditions in the dome, and the plans being made to try to take what we have here." Byl and Aaron stopped eating since this was the first they had heard of this.

Byl said, "They don't have any idea what we have here, do they? Since no one has been outside the dome, all they probably know is that we exist. They certainly don't know that virtually every adult here is a skilled hunter, adept with a longbow and crossbow." He turned to Nathan. "What kinds of weapons do they have in the dome?"

Nathan thought a minute. "I've never really seen any weapons. The police aren't armed with guns since crime is relatively unheard of. In a confined space, everyone knows each other, and there's no place to hide. Nightsticks—heavy clubs—are about the only thing I've seen them carry."

Aaron joined in. "I'm guessing they have a stash of old weaponry left over from before the Great War. I'm also guessing that it's probably in pretty bad shape, and any ammunition that was left would also be suspect."

Sam agreed with Aaron. "You're probably right about the old weapons, but if this government has been operating in some degree of secrecy, there's always the possibility that they have somehow maintained operational weapons or possibly designed new ones."

Nathan thought about the idea of new weapons, or even maintaining old ones. "I don't think they would be able to develop anything new, and it would be difficult to invest a lot in maintaining old weapons. I hear what my mom has to say about the water purifiers and air handlers, and they barely have enough resources to keep them operational. I mean, unless the government really didn't care about the people in the dome and was willing to divert resources from the maintenance of life support systems—" Nathan stopped in mid-thought. Everyone looked at him, waiting for him to continue. After a moment, he added, "Actually, knowing what I know now, I guess there is a possibility that the government is doing that. If they think it might be safe to move outside the dome and that there are resources out here waiting to be taken, perhaps investing in weapons and letting the infrastructure of the dome degrade isn't such a far-fetched idea."

The discussion stopped at that point, and everyone settled into eating dinner. Nathan loved all the new flavors and had seconds on every dish. As he was finishing the last pieces of pineapple, he decided to ask a question that had been bothering him ever since he first saw Honoli'i. "I'm the only person in the dome that looks like me, yet here in Honoli'i, everyone looks like me. Why? How could this come about?"

Sam looked at each person seated around the room. "Well, I think I can provide part of the answer, and I can also guess at another part. After the Great War, the people who lived in Honoli'i thought the worst was over, but it wasn't. Small amounts of radiation continued to drift over from Oahu, and many people died from radiation sickness. It's my understanding that almost one-third of the population died. However, the radiation wasn't through with Honoli'i yet. From what people could determine—and part of this is conjecture since there really weren't any scientific laboratories here, or anywhere close by for that matter—a virus mutated in such a way that it was able to deliver its altered genes to human cells, a process called transduction."

Byl jumped in here. "They tell us in our schools that the virus caused people to become extremely ill, suffering from high temperatures and dehydration. It was so bad that at least half of the people who survived the radiation sickness died from the viral infection. There were so many bodies that the inability to dispose of them led to the spread of other diseases. Apparently, the stench was so bad that—" Byl stopped and looked around at everyone seated. "Oops, sorry to be so graphic at dinner."

Sam continued, "Not only—as Byl so graphically described—did people die, but the virus changed them in a very dramatic way. It seems that the transduction replaced certain genes on the chromosomes of the survivors, eliminating all the varieties of genes for hair color and eye color and replacing them entirely with genes for blond hair and green eyes. Every child born to the survivors after the viral attack had those traits. That is supposedly why we all look alike here in Honoliʻi." Everyone seated looked around at everyone else, as if they had never noticed this characteristic before.

"As we all know, the virus altered some other things in the population. Every child was also born without a developed larynx and had the ability to, what we now call, thalk. There are probably some other more subtle changes that occurred, but these are certainly the most obvious ones."

Nathan's mind was racing as he tried to figure out what this meant as far as he was concerned. He was the only person in the dome who had blond hair and green eyes. He was the only person in the dome without a larynx and who could thalk. How could this have happened? As usual, everyone seated knew exactly what was on his mind. Nathan looked at Sam, hoping for an explanation.

"Well, Nathan, this is the part I can only guess at. It could be that the virus entered the dome, possibly through the submarine fishing operation, or it came in through the air filtration system. Since your parents are both in contact with these portions of dome operations that have direct contact with the outside, it would be logical that they would be the ones affected and not others."

Sam paused here. "Or …"

Nathan leaned forward. "Or what?"

Sam took in a deep breath. "Remember when I told you about the *waʻa kaukahi* that was pulled into the cave when the fishing pen was harvested?" Nathan nodded.

"You were the baby in the boat."

PART 2
Growing

11
Three Years Later

Nathan's hunger intensified, gnawing at him like some ravenous beast from within, as he watched Layla and Auntie Bernice place the settings for the evening meal. The gathering in the Pahinui *hale* was similar to the first dinner Nathan had in Honoli'i three years ago, but once again, this event was to celebrate the anniversary of his arrival, one of the things he looked forward to every year. He could not believe the time had passed so quickly, and that he had become so thoroughly involved with life in the village since leaving the dome.

Instead of school with regular classes, textbooks, and homework, Nathan lived his lessons. His new teachers excelled in the subjects they taught and eagerly passed on the skills they had honed through years of practice and experience. Kayli, Byl, and Aaron, experts in the use of the longbow and crossbow, were amazed at how quickly Nathan became adept at using the weapons. As soon as he was proficient with both, Kayli took it upon herself to show Nathan how to navigate through the dense forest by finding animal paths, stalk his prey, and then dispatch the animal with one shot. Unlike the boar that attacked Nathan, a missed first shot would alert the prey to danger, and a second shot was rarely possible. The people of Honoli'i fully accepted Nathan as a member of the community when they came to realize that he was providing the village with many of the *pua'a* and wild goats that ended up in Edward Park's butcher shop.

Sam Pahinui, along with his two sons, taught Nathan the ancient art of building and handling an outrigger canoe. Rowing the craft out to the breakers that revealed the location of submerged reefs for fishing excursions added bulk to Nathan's upper body, and a growth spurt over the years resulted in his being a full head taller than Kayli. Nathan was no longer the bookish schoolboy that was swept out of Hilo by the Wailuku River.

Fishing was one of Nathan's favorite pastimes. The fish on the reef were plentiful, and the varieties were astounding. Sam showed Nathan how to chew *kukui* nuts to extract the oil. If the water was calm, Nathan learned that if a person spits the oil onto the surface of the water, the reflections clear away, revealing the location of schools of fish. In addition to using a line and hook, Sam showed Nathan how to use a cast net in the shallows between the reef and the beach. Throwing the net so that it splayed out flat over the water in a perfect circle, allowing the weighted edge to sink and entrap the fish below, was a special skill, one that Nathan honed to perfection.

One of the things Nathan really liked to catch was *tako*. Kayli taught him how to make lures out of cowry shells—temptations an octopus could not pass up. He also enjoyed hunting for them at night in the shallow reef by the village. *Tako* were much more aggressive at night and actively stalked the reef. Kayli and he would get *kukui* nut torches, wade out in the reef, and wait patiently with their spears. His favorite thing to do with the octopus was to make *tako kim chee poke*.

Finally, Layla and Auntie Bernice insisted that everyone, both boys and girls, must know how to cook. They showed Nathan how to dig an *imu*, use *ti* and banana leaves as wrappings to keep foods moist, and to grill meats without burning them. Nathan was particularly proud of the fact that for this dinner, Bernie had allowed him to prepare her specialty—grilled goat skewers.

The educational process was not all one-way. Nathan used the few books that were available in Honoli'i to teach Kayli, Byl, and Aaron how to read. He also took their basic math skills, satisfactory for local commerce and trading, and taught them rudimentary geometry and algebra. All the members of the family loved to compare the history they knew from word-of-mouth with the knowledge Nathan had gained from texts he used in school. In many cases, the stories did not quite match up, resulting in some good-natured disputes, and in the end, the participants simply had to agree to disagree.

One of the skills Nathan possessed that surprised the Pahinui family the most was Nathan's ability to play the guitar. He had never mentioned it. They first heard him play about two years ago when they had been at a big village picnic, and someone was playing as people ate. Nathan asked to borrow the musician's guitar and stunned them all by playing beautiful songs that none of them had ever heard. Byl, Aaron, and Kayli all wanted to learn, so Sam scoured the village for instruments to buy. Nathan began giving them lessons, and it was soon very evident that all the Pahinuis were naturally talented at playing.

The days were so crammed with activities that the only time Nathan had for reflection was late in the evening as he tossed and turned in a futile attempt to sleep; it seemed like torture to him. Alone in his bed, thoughts of his parents and his former life in the dome raced through his head, sometimes driving him to tears. The uncertainty surrounding his parents' safety, and the knowledge that they must be horribly upset by his disappearance, made the nights almost unbearable. Nathan could only hope that they were okay as they continued on with life in Hilo.

***

Several days after the anniversary dinner, Nathan was alone in the shallows using his cast net to get fish for that evening's dinner. In the distance, he could see a small outrigger containing two men navigate through the gaps in the reef, alternately paddling and surfing the boat towards the shore. He soon realized it was Byl and Aaron, but he could not figure out why they seemed to be in such a hurry, paddling aggressively between each wave. As they neared the shore, they hopped out of the canoe and began to drag it up on to the beach. Nathan pulled in his net and raced over to help.

Nathan said, "Hey, guys, what's the rush? You could have caught a few more waves and let them bring you in without all that work."

Byl, very much out of breath, said, "You're not going to believe what we saw. We were poaching a few fish from the *kāhala* pens when we saw part of the dome walls surrounding Hilo begin to open, just north of where the Wailuku comes out into the bay!"

Aaron joined in. "We stopped what we were doing and started watching very carefully. As the panel of the dome seemed to slide open, several people totally covered in white suits and helmets with visors came out and started to walk towards the bay. We ducked behind Coconut Island, so I don't think they noticed us."

"They didn't stay along the bay for very long," said Byl. "After a few minutes, they started to make their way along the outside of the dome, heading up towards the falls and into the forest. When we lost sight of them, we decided to make a break for home." He took a deep breath. "Now, we need to get up to the village and let Dad know what we saw." Nathan helped the two brothers pull the outrigger up out of the water, and the three of them raced up the path to Honoliʻi.

The boys finally located Sam in Edward Park's butcher shop. After they described what they saw, Sam and Edward considered the possibilities.

"It could be a small repair party sent out to examine a damaged section of the dome," Edward suggested.

Sam nodded, but added, "That's possible, or it could be an exploratory group to see if it's safe for a larger contingent to follow."

Nathan was intrigued. "You could be right, Sam. It could be the start of what I heard Chief Teshima and Mayor Hapuna talking about the day I got chased and swept out into the bay. They may be exploring the possibility of sending men out to get rid of people living outside the dome."

"Well, if this is the beginning of something that could lead to a possible conflict with the people of Honoli'i," Sam said, "we better get over there to check it out."

Sam and Edward left the shop and quickly organized a small group of men to carefully scout out the situation. Sam told Nathan to let the family know where he went and instructed Byl and Aaron to get their crossbows to accompany him on the scouting mission. Nathan was disappointed that he was not asked to go along but went to find Kayli and the others as Sam had asked.

Moving silently through the forest, communicating without a spoken word, the scouting party from Honoli'i moved across the plateau. It did not take long for the men to arrive at the upper reaches of the Wailuku, about one hundred meters above where it entered the dome. From their high vantage point, the men could catch glimpses of the men from Hilo as they moved around the rim of the dome. They could also eavesdrop on their conversations, making it unnecessary to move in for a closer visual inspection.

"The grating protecting the turbine blades that generate the electricity for the entire dome is actually inside the enclosure. We can clean away debris that accumulates there without coming outside. Recently, however, one of the large metal struts that are situated along the outer-most edge of the dome was found lodged at the bottom of the grating. It had broken away, probably hit by a large limb that sheared off a tree upriver. You can see where rust and corrosion have eaten through many of the supportive struts that keep these larger chunks of wood out."

Another voice asked, "If we need to replace or strengthen these struts, do we have to come outside to make the repairs?"

The first man responded, "No, we don't have to come outside to do that simply because we *can't* do that. We don't have the materials or technology to forge metal like this and then weld it into place." There was a minute of silence before the man continued, "You are the officers of our security force. I'm showing you this to convince you that we will no longer be able to stay isolated in the dome. We are losing our ability to provide the resources necessary to sustain our population, and the dome itself is in danger. We will, sooner rather than later, need to expand outward."

A third voice joined in. "Chief Teshima, I assume that is why we have been taking air and soil samples, along with radiation counts, as we've been moving along outside the dome; we need to see if it's safe to live out here."

Sam looked at Byl, who was standing close beside him. "Chief Teshima? That's one of the men Nathan told us about when he first arrived. He's responsible for the security pursuit that forced Nathan to jump into the Wailuku."

Teshima responded to the man's comment, "That's correct. We have long suspected that it is now safe out here. We are wearing these suits as a precaution, but I think in the future, they may not be necessary. Further analysis of these samples will tell us more. However, environmental hazards are not the only threats out here. We anticipate encountering a native population of Ferals as we move outwards. I want you to start weapons training for all of your men because I suspect that these Ferals will be quite hostile towards us since we shut them out of the dome's protection during and after the Great War. If that is the case, they will need to be subdued. I can't stress this threat strongly enough. I think we need to shoot first and ask questions later."

"Weapons training? All we have are these nightsticks. It won't take much training to handle these."

Teshima chuckled. "You will not be using the nightsticks out here. The mayor and I have been setting aside some of the dome's resources to maintain a cache of old weapons that were designed around the time of the Great War. They fire a burst of electric power that is accurate to about twenty meters, and can stun or kill a man, depending on the setting. Watch."

Sam and the scouting party could not see Teshima pull the small pistol from his protective suit, but they could hear the sizzle of an electric discharge and the crack of a small explosion as the charge charred the trunk of a nearby mulberry tree.

"Well, gentlemen, pretty impressive, don't you think? As long as we have the turbines generating electricity, we can keep them charged. However, as you can see from the struts here, time is of the essence. Let's head back inside to discuss the training schedule and to have these soil and water samples analyzed."

As they turned to go, a bolt—or short arrow—released from a crossbow whistled through the forest and struck one of Teshima's men squarely in the back. With a startled look on his face, the man pitched forward, landing at Teshima's feet. When Teshima bent down to see if the man was alive, he could tell from the frothy, bright red blood oozing from his mouth that if he wasn't dead now, he would be in a few minutes. Teshima said to the remaining men, "Quickly, we need to get back into the dome!" He turned to the man closest to him. "You. Help me drag this guy in with us. Don't pull out the arrow; it will only increase the bleeding—not that I think he has a chance anyway."

Sam was confused as the men from the dome attempted a retreat. It took him several minutes to realize one of the men had been hit with a bolt shot from a crossbow, and that all of the men in his scouting party were accounted for and too far away through dense forest to have dealt the deadly shot. Where did it come from?

"Quiet! Stay hidden!" Sam said.

As they watched Teshima's party scurry back inside, Sam knew that they were not alone on the hillside overlooking the waterfall.

12
Captured

Abe Hasegawa and Michael Wai were back near Hilo Dome on their second spy mission. Kawananakoa wanted more precise information about the dome's vulnerabilities since he wanted that to be his first conquest on the windward side. Abe and Michael had just received that information from overhearing Chief Teshima himself. Kawananakoa also wanted to stir up a little trouble to help set the stage for an attack.

"Pretty good shot, Michael," Abe Hasegawa whispered to Michael Wai as they watched Teshima and his men retreat back into the dome. "I couldn't have done better myself! We need to stay hidden until they close the dome back up; then we can get back to our camp to let Kawananakoa know we accomplished our mission. He'll be very pleased to know that we have set in motion a plan that should lead to a direct conflict between Honoli'i and Hilo." He smiled. "And to think it will be all over a little misunderstanding about who killed one of their men."

Michael smiled back at Abe, saying nothing. He was, in fact, quite proud of his marksmanship, and he planned to let Kawananakoa know exactly who fired the fatal arrow. They watched as the panel slid into place on the dome, once again sealing Hilo off from the rest of the world. It was time to head out. What they did not realize was that Sam and his men had picked up their whispered conversation and were now waiting for them to make the next move.

Using thalk, Sam directed his men to work in pairs and to spread out across the forest in the direction he anticipated the two assassins would take. Based on what Abe had said, he was fairly certain there were only two men and that they had to be hidden somewhere below. They had to be down close to the dome in order to have made the successful kill shot. Stealth was of the essence for his group of men since he also believed that the two would not suspect that they were about to encounter other people in the forest. Surprise was necessary for his patrol to have the advantage.

Michael and Abe began to make their way across the hillside through the dense vegetation, looking for the small *pua'a* trail that brought them down to the dome, close enough to complete the mission. They quickly found the trail and began the climb uphill. The path twisted and curved so that visibility directly ahead was extremely limited. After climbing about fifty meters, the path took a sharp turn to the left, and as they rounded the curve, they were confronted by Byl and Aaron, each with a crossbow aimed directly at them.

Abe and Michael froze even though no command was given. The blond hair of the men confronting them sent a clear message; they were facing people from Honoli'i. Were they looking at hunters who encountered them accidently, or had they been hunted, just as they had stalked Teshima's men? After a silent stand-off of what seemed like five minutes—but actually lasted just a few seconds—one of the men lowered his crossbow and motioned them to come forward.

As soon as Michael saw Byl lower his weapon, he spun around and began to race back down the *pua'a* path using Abe's body as a screen. Abe realized he was being set up as a shield and dropped to a crouch; he had no intention of taking a crossbow bolt for his fleeing friend. With a clear shot, Aaron pulled the trigger, sending the short arrow on its way. As Michael cried out in pain, Abe placed his own crossbow carefully on the ground and stood slowly with his hands raised. Looking down the hill, he could see Michael lying motionless just off the path, face down with a short arrow sticking out from between his shoulder blades. Abe turned and cautiously approached the two men, one of whom kept a loaded crossbow pointed directly at him.

When Abe got close, Byl pulled out some cord, motioned Abe to turn around, and tied Abe's hands securely behind him. What Abe could not hear was Aaron's thalk message to his father. "Dad, we have one of the shooters secured. The other one tried to run, so I had to shoot him." Aaron hesitated, trying to control his emotions. "Dad, I think I killed him. I didn't think I would ever have to do something like that, but I also didn't think we could let him escape."

Hearing the concern in his son's thoughts, Sam said, "You did the right thing, Aaron. You acted quickly, but not irresponsibly. Don't check on the person you shot; I'll do that. Hold your prisoner there until I arrive with the rest of the men. I'm glad that you are both okay. And you're correct; we really couldn't allow him to escape not knowing what they were here for."

As Abe waited with his two captors, he began to think about how Kawananakoa would not get to know the outcome of their mission. Although the plan was successfully executed to elevate tensions between the people of Hilo and the people of Honoliʻi with the expectation of leading them into direct conflict, his leader would have no idea that this occurred. Kawananakoa would probably have to send out yet another team of spies, and the timing of the whole operation would be thrown off. What Abe did not realize was that Byl, Aaron, and the rest of the scouting party from Honoliʻi were listening to his thoughts, just as if he were confessing the whole plot directly to them.

***

Upon entering the dome, Teshima immediately stepped out of his protective suit, directed his lieutenant to make arrangements for contacting the dead security guard's family, and headed for the mayor's office. Brushing aside his guard's salutes as he entered the building, he made for the steps, taking them two at a time to the second floor. As he entered the outer part of the office, the mayor's secretary looked up. "Chief Teshima, I'll let the mayor know—" But she was unable to finish her sentence as Teshima blew by her.

Mayor Hapuna looked up as Teshima threw open the door and entered his office. "Well, Chief, how did your little demonstration go?"

"They attacked us!"

"What? Who attacked you?"

"I have to assume it was those damn Ferals. Who else could it be? I concluded my demonstration of our electronic pistol, we turned to head back into the dome, and one of our men took a crossbow bolt right in the back."

Mayor Hapuna pushed his chair back from the desk and stood up slowly. "Did anyone else get hurt?"

"No, we dragged the body back into the dome as quickly as possible. I have my lieutenant notifying the family now."

Hapuna thought for a moment. "Well, this is going to accelerate our plans. However, it certainly gives us the opening we need to go on the offensive. The news of this will spread very quickly throughout the dome. It should be easy to convince the general public that the time has come to wipe out the Ferals to take what we need if we want to continue to survive here on Hawaii, and that we will be the ones who can lead them through this difficult time."

Teshima said, "I think you're right, but we still need a lot more time for getting our weapons in order and for training. Also, if they have crossbows, we'll have difficulty getting in range to be effective with our guns. I think we are going to have to manufacture our own bows and get the men trained in using them as well." Teshima paused. "We might also think about instituting a draft. We really have no idea about how many of them are out there."

Hapuna said, "Okay, start by redirecting some of our environmental maintenance staff to begin making the crossbows. If we're planning to leave the dome, we really don't need them to spend all their time working on equipment we're going to abandon anyway. I'll start preparing a speech to address the general public informing them of our increased state of emergency and the need to make some personal sacrifices for the good of the community. I won't mention a draft, yet, but I will say that we are approaching a state of war as a result of this cowardly and unwarranted attack on our people."

Teshima looked doubtful. "This will take some time," he cautioned.

"Yes, I know," Hapuna said. "So, why are you still here? I suggest you better get on it, right now."

Teshima was not sure he liked the tone in Hapuna's voice, and he also did not like taking a direct order from someone he regarded as his equal in the power structure. Teshima also resented the fact that he did all the hard work while Hapuna sat in his office doing nothing. However, there was nothing he could do about it—for now. Keeping his anger in, he turned and left the office without further comment.

***

Kayli watched Nathan as he paced anxiously back and forth in front of their *hale*. She, too, was disappointed that she was not included in the group that left to observe the activity at the dome, but at this point, there was nothing that could be done about it.

"Why don't you come sit down instead of wearing a trench in front of our door?"

Nathan stopped and gave her a dirty look. "How can you just sit there? The suspense is killing me, especially since this concerns my home. I should have been included in the group since I know more about the place than anyone in the village."

Kayli thought about this for a minute, and then said, "Yes, that's true, but if our people are spotted by anyone from the dome, it's better that you're not there. You could be recognized."

Nathan considered what she had said and then shook his head. "I look so different now that I doubt anyone would make the connection. After all, it's been years since I left."

"That's true, also, but—" Kayli stopped in mid-sentence. "Wait. I think I sense them returning."

They both turned to look towards the path leading out of the village, and in a moment, the small band of men from Honoli'i appeared at the edge of the forest. Sam was in the lead, with Byl and Aaron not far behind with the others, but between the two of them stumbled a young man with dark hair that stood out like a piece of lava rock on a white sandy beach. His hands were behind his back, and it soon became obvious he was a prisoner. Nathan and Kayli raced out to meet them.

Abe was confused as he saw the boy and girl run towards the group. Not a word had been spoken since his capture, yet everyone seemed to know what to do and acted in a very coordinated way. *They are either very well trained*, he thought, *or they have some unique way of communicating. Maybe hand signals of some kind?* In any case, it was obvious there was no way he was going to be able to escape, especially as he thought back to what had happened to Michael.

Kayli and Nathan walked alongside Sam as they continued toward the center of town. Sam had a very stern look about him and did not readily offer any explanations. Finally, Kayli said, "So, who's our reluctant visitor?"

At first, Kayli did not think her father was going to respond. Finally, he said, "We captured him as he and another man tried to leave the dome area. One of the two shot a dome guard with a crossbow, probably killing him. Aaron and Byl ambushed them as they were trying to make their way back up the mountain. In the process, one of them made a break to escape being taken prisoner. Your brother, Aaron, had to shoot him to prevent him from getting away. Let's just say our prisoner's partner won't be joining us."

Kayli looked over at Aaron as they continued to walk towards the village center. He glanced at her, then looked away. "I had to do it, Kayli. If he had escaped, he would have returned to wherever he came from, probably Cook, with information that could prove harmful to us and our village. It wasn't something I wanted to do, or even thought about before doing it; it was simply a reflexive action."

"And he did the right thing," Sam added. "This whole situation is now going to require some careful and serious analysis to see what the impact will be on our relationship with the government inside the dome. I'm afraid it could set things in motion that will lead to a direct and combative interaction."

A small crowd of people gathered in the center of the village to see what was going on. They all "heard" the exchange that just occurred and looked anxiously at one another, trying to perceive what it might all mean for them. As the procession stopped just in front of them, Sam, Edward Park, and several other men stepped away from the group. "Now that we have him, what are we going to do with him?" Sam said as he nodded towards the prisoner. "It's not like we have a jail in which we can hold him. Plus, how can we even interrogate him? We can't talk, and he can't hear us 'thalk.'"

Hearing this, Nathan thought he might be able to help. "Sam, maybe he can read. If I write out questions we want to ask him, we might be able to get some kind of response out of him, either through what he thinks or what he actually says, which of course, may be two entirely different things if he tells lies but thinks the truth."

Sam thought about it for a minute. "Well, it's a long shot, but we may as well give it a try. I can't think of any other way to get through to him." He looked over at Byl and Aaron. "Take him into the town hall and tie him to the center pole in the main room. Edward, please organize a rotating watch schedule with some of the men since we don't have a room secure enough to hold him. I'm not sure how long we will have to "entertain" our guest, so you may have to have quite a few men on the schedule. Nathan, let's go back home to see how we're going to approach the questioning."

By the time Aaron and Byl arrived back at the Pahinui *hale*, Sam, Kayli, and Nathan were already seated in the living area discussing the questions to be asked.

"Perhaps we should keep it simple," Nathan suggested, "just to see if he can read at all, maybe just "name" with a question mark."

Kayli said, "How about "live?" since he might get confused as to whether it means staying alive or where he lives. Either way, he'll have to think about the word, and we can determine that he at least is able to read."

"We already know why they were here and what the general plan was as far as killing one of the guards was concerned," said Aaron, looking at Byl for confirmation. "That's what he was thinking about while we held him waiting for you to arrive."

Byl nodded. "He's right, but what we need to know is where Kawananakoa is now, how many people are with him, and what they plan to do once they get here."

"And," added Sam, "what was he going to report back on and how would it influence Kawananakoa's actions."

Sam looked at them, paused for a moment, and said, "Well, that's good for starters. We can take it further if, in fact, he does know how to read. I'm still skeptical about that. We'll start with two words suggested by Nathan and Kayli, then follow up with the others if we get a positive response. Agreed?"

Everyone nodded their approval, and then they set off for the center of town.

13
On the March

Alfred Kawananakoa was becoming more impatient with each day that passed without any news from his spies, especially Michael Wai and Abe Hasegawa. His army had made fairly slow progress from Cook as they wound around South Point and began the climb up to the Kilauea Crater. The volcano had been quiet since the last eruption, the one that buried much of their fertile land and scattered their livestock, but the plume of smoke and steam that continued from the inner crater of Hale Mau Mau was a constant reminder of the peril they all faced living on the volatile mountain.

The small villages of Naahelu and Pahala, located just past South Point, were easy enough to conquer, and both towns had enough fruit, vegetables, and feral goats and pigs to keep his army fed. The plentiful macadamia nuts there provided the men with an additional source of protein when the game became scarce, as it often did. Kawananakoa was also able to conscript many of the men from these villages into his army, pressing them into service against their will and leaving their families without able-bodied workers and hunters. Kamehameha VI, as he now liked to call himself, did not leave a great deal of goodwill in his wake.

The travel itself had not been difficult, following the remnants of the Hawaii Belt Road, old Route 11, had made the going easy, and within a few months, Kawananakoa and his army found themselves on the rim of Kilauea Crater. However, the weather at the crater was damp and chilly, and several of the men, unused to such conditions, became ill and died. With nasty weather and little there to eat, Kawananakoa quickly began the trek down the side of the mountain, heading for what he hoped would be their final destination—Hilo.

Kawananakoa brought his march to a halt in the remnants of a village once known as Keaau. From there, he sent his spies out to gather information about Hilo and the surrounding area, and a scouting team to find a suitable place to launch a sea attack. Strategically located, Keaau was an easy two-day march to Hilo, and about the same distance from the deserted village of Hāʻena, located alongside a sheltered cove and beach. He had learned of the existence of Keaau and Hā'ena from previous spy expeditions, and although they were in the right place for an attack, they had very little to offer in the way of food. For this reason, he needed information from his spies as soon as possible.

The scouting team returned and confirmed what he had already anticipated—Hā'ena was the perfect launch site. The coast was relatively calm and located around a point that was the eastern edge of Hilo Bay. It would be a long row across some rough and dangerous seas, but it was nothing new to the men he had selected to crew the boats. They were accustomed to the waters that pounded the lava sea cliffs along the coastline below Cook. The army from Cook settled in and went to work on building the boats they would need for the attack, not knowing that one of their spies was dead, and the other about to undergo interrogation.

***

When Sam, Nathan, and Kayli arrived at the town hall, they found Abe Hasegawa tied securely to the main post. Edward Park had done a good job, using *kaula* made from *olonā*, one of the most prized fibers for use in fishing lines and nets, as well as in weaponry. There was no way Abe would be able to break away, but as instructed, Edward had arranged a watch schedule to keep an eye on the prisoner. Nathan had written the two words, "name?" and "live" on some scraps of paper, and after glancing at Sam and Kayli, moved in front of the prisoner. He was a bit nervous since he was not sure this would get a good response, if any. Sam directed Nathan to show the prisoner the first word: "Name?"

Nathan held the paper up an arm's distance from the prisoner's face. Abe glanced first at Nathan and then focused on the paper. His first thought was, *What's this charade all about?* Some disappointment registered on Nathan's face, but then he sensed the word "Abe" emanating from the prisoner. Nathan nodded his head vigorously. The prisoner said, "My name is Abe Hasegawa."

Nathan held up the second word: "Live." He sensed confusion in Abe's thoughts, and with a piece of charcoal added the word: "Where?" "Cook" immediately popped into Abe's thoughts, and then after a brief pause, he said aloud, "Cook." Nathan again nodded approval.

Sam motioned for Nathan, Kayli, Byl, Aaron, and Ed to gather in one corner of the town hall.

He said, "Well, we know he can read some words, but what should we do now that we know this?"

Byl chimed in, "Well, as I said when we captured him, we need to know where Kawananakoa is now, how many people are with him, and what they plan to do once they get here."

Kayli said, "How about some simple prompts. He doesn't actually have to tell us the answers; all he has to do is start to think about them. In his thought process, we may be able to extract what we need. And, since he is not fully aware of our capabilities, what he is thinking is likely to be true."

Aaron suggested, "Let's continue to keep it simple. "Where live?" worked, so let's try "Where Kawananakoa?" It might get him thinking." He looked around the small groups and saw everyone nodding in agreement.

Nathan wrote out another sign and again confronted Abe. Abe's first reaction was, *How do they know about Kawananakoa?* Nathan pulled the sign away and went back over to Sam and the rest of the group. Nathan said, "I think this is going to be like fishing; we put out the bait and then wait for some action."

But, like any good fishing spot, they did not have to wait long for some nibbles. They could tell that Abe was beginning to panic just a bit. His thoughts were running through his head faster than *ahi* in the open ocean. *I can't tell them about my rendezvous plans. They can't find out that Kawananakoa may already be in Keaau. The whole outrigger attack from Hāʻena would be compromised. If I ever do escape and get back, and Kawananakoa finds out I coughed everything up, I'm as dead as my so-called buddy Michael. I'll just play dumb. Haha! Dumb, like them not talking. They know I can read a bit, but they don't know how good I am at it. What if they torture me? I won't talk; I won't give up our attack plans.*

Sam thalked to the group, "Well, that tells us just about everything except how many there are. We may have to do a little spy mission of our own to see what's going on near Hāʻena. The problem is, I don't think anyone from our village has ever been over to that area of the island. Could be tricky not knowing what it's like."

Byl and Aaron, without even looking at each other, thalked, "We'll be glad to do that!"

Sam looked doubtful. "Don't you think you guys have done enough? I'm very proud of you for what you have accomplished already; maybe it's time for some others to step up." Sam looked around the group.

Nathan said, "I can go. I think I'm ready to take on this kind of assignment."

Sam looked at him quite carefully and said, "Actually, there's something I have in mind for you that involves your knowledge of the Hilo dome. I'd rather have you close by than on the other side of the structure."

Kayli was about to volunteer, and sensing this, Sam gave her a quick look and said, "I think it would be best for you to team up with Nathan. It would be best to have the two of you for what I have planned. Okay. Byl and Aaron, let's make some plans. There are some logistical measures we have to consider with a mission such as this."

***

Kawananakoa was not happy with what he was discovering as he and his men made their way from Keaau to Hā'ena. To launch from Hā'ena, he was counting on finding enough mature *koa* trees near the shore to make large, double outrigger canoes known as *wa'a kaulua*. These canoes could carry more men and would be much more stable in an open-ocean transit. Unfortunately for Kawananakoa, *koa* grows best at higher altitudes. He had seen large stands of these valuable trees as they moved through the volcano area, but as they descended to Keaau, they became fewer and fewer. Smaller, single hull canoes, known as *wa'a kaukahi*, held fewer men and were not as stable in the open water. It would be possible to use a different tree, such as a *kukui* nut, but the wood is lighter and therefore not as stable in the water. Kawananakoa knew from his scouts that there were many macadamia nut trees nearby left from a huge plantation that had been abandoned long ago. However, although the nuts might provide some food, the trunks were not suitable for making canoes. In any event, locating appropriate trees, cutting them and getting the logs to the shore, and finally finishing the production with hand tools such as the *ko'i* adze in a *halau* (canoe shed) would be an arduous and time-consuming process. His crew had done this while they lived in Cook, but in Cook there were plenty of men and good tools. This was certainly not the case in Hā'ena. *Well*, Kawananakoa thought, *all we can do is buckle down and get to it.*

14
Meetings and Preparations

Chief Howard Teshima sat at the head of a long table in one of the meeting rooms of the old Federal Building. He looked at the dozen government employees he had asked to meet with him. It was not going to be an easy discussion. It was Chief Teshima's task to let these employees know that conditions were going to continue to get worse, not better. He was very annoyed that Hapuna was not doing this. It technically was his job. However, if all these people viewed him as the leader, it might be easier if, and when, he needed to push Hapuna out of the way. But for now, Teshima had to try to get them to understand that a drastic change would have to be made in the way Hilo Dome existed. The dome would have to open.

Lora Ohana, as the official in charge of the dome environmental conditions, along with her husband, Jonathan, as the one responsible for the fish farming operations out of Coconut Island, were both present at the meeting. As they surveyed the room, they realized that all the people seated at the table were division leaders of some kind—farming, electricity, roads and bridges, buildings, and communications. The light chatter of conversations stopped as Teshima cleared his throat.

"I would like to thank you all for coming here today. I know it's difficult to get everyone to clear their schedules to meet at the same time; I want you to know that I really appreciate that. As many of you are aware, the conditions in the dome are deteriorating, and we do not have the resources to keep up with the maintenance. Many of the mechanicals, especially for critical factors such as air, water, and food production, have been receiving the majority of our maintenance efforts, and rightfully so."

Lora and Jonathan looked at each other, both thinking the same thing. They had been under close surveillance by Teshima and his men in the years following Nathan's disappearance into the swirling waters of the Wailuku. They had been held captive for a day as both Mayor Hapuna and Chief Teshima interrogated them about what they thought Nathan had discovered, but it was quickly discerned that they knew nothing. They were allowed to return home and were given two weeks off to grieve for their son before they had to return to their jobs, jobs that were critical to the survival of the Hilo Dome community. The conditions of their release were that they would never divulge what had actually happened. Nathan had an "accident," and that was that. Their hatred for Teshima and Hapuna never decreased, but they had other things to think about as they went about their daily lives doing their jobs.

Teshima continued, oblivious to their thoughts. "What many of you do not know is that a few days ago, while on a survey mission to sample the air, water, and soil outside the dome, and to inspect the protective grating that shields our turbine blades from debris in the water entering the dome, one of our men was shot." He paused. "Shot in the back by someone with a crossbow." There were murmurs around the table as the import of this struck home (much like the crossbow bolt that killed Teshima's man). "We were unable to save him, and we were unable to determine just who fired the shot. But what we do know is that the Ferals are hostile, just as we had feared."

"Why is this important to know?" Teshima looked around the table. It was a rhetorical question, as far as he was concerned, because he was about to tell them the answer. "It is important to know this because, as I said earlier to start this meeting, conditions are deteriorating." He paused again to look at their faces. "To put it simply, we are going to have to open Hilo Dome."

After a stunned momentary silence, a cacophony of questions erupted from around the table. Lora was finally able to get everyone's attention.

"As the person in charge of environmental control, my primary concern is centered on the safety of our citizens. I am assuming that your test results have indicated that there are no lingering environmental problems associated with the radiation from the war."

"That is correct, Lora," said Teshima. "As far as soil, water, and air are concerned, it is safe. But as I just described, there is a hostile environment that exists right outside our walls. And before we can open up the dome, it must be dealt with."

Jonathan asked, "By dealt with, do you mean through aggressive actions, such as attacking the Ferals? Do we have the resources to do that? Weapons? Personnel?"

"Good questions, Jonathan. To address these needs, the mayor and I have decided to implement a draft, of sorts, to augment our security force. This means that some of our citizens will have to leave some of the tasks they would normally be doing to receive training in tactics and the use of weapons. We will also be diverting some of our physical resources towards the production of weapons." Teshima paused once again as the people around the table erupted. "Please, everyone, remain calm! We are all in this together!"

Andrew Sun, head of communications, had remained silent through most of this. Now, he felt that he needed to be heard. "Since it is safe to go outside the dome, don't you think some more research needs to be done concerning the Ferals? Are they really hostile towards us, or was this some rogue individual acting out on his own? Where are they located, and how many of them are there? I don't think we can act blindly on this. What if, on the whole, they are a peaceful group? We could be instigating hostilities that could escalate into an all-out war. In fact, if they have been existing outside our dome for all these years, they may have survival skills that would be of great value to us."

"Don't be naïve," Teshima sneered. "They have already initiated the hostilities. We have to assume the worst." He looked around the table at everyone. "While the mayor and I appreciate your input, the decision has been made. We are moving forward with our plans to train people and produce weapons in order to prepare for an attack on the Ferals. Dissention will not be tolerated when it comes to our survival strategies. Am I clear on this?"

A stunned silence followed his remarks. Teshima smiled. "Good. I'm glad we are all in agreement. As you might expect, none of what was discussed today can be made public until we have everything in place, especially for the draft. Please go about your duties. We will contact each of you as plans are developed regarding your particular areas of responsibility in the dome."

"You are dismissed." He pushed back his chair, stood, and with a short bow, turned and exited the room.

Lora was the first to speak. "Well, I guess we need to get back to our jobs, but I think we all need to get behind this effort the best we can." The whole time she was saying this, she was shaking her head and motioning for everyone to start leaving the conference room. She was almost certain there was at least one hidden microphone in the room and that Teshima and Hapuna were listening in to hear their reactions to Teshima's presentation. "Jonathan and I are going for lunch over at the L & L if anyone wants to come along with us."

Most of the others made comments agreeing with Lora and said they would join them at the L & L.

As expected, later at the L & L, everybody reassembled, ordered some plate lunches, pushed some tables together into a corner of the diner, and sat down to have a quiet discussion about what was to follow. Andrew Sun, a small, quiet man, had a determined look on his face as he cut into his chicken-*kāhala lau lau*. He looked around the diner to make sure no one else was listening except his fellow administrators at the table. "I meant what I said back in the conference room. We need to investigate this further. I don't like the idea of literally going off half-cocked launching an aggressive action against people—and they are people, people who may not be war-like in nature at all!"

Jonathan pushed around the chicken long rice on his plate as he considered Andrew's reiteration of his stance. "I agree with Andrew. The question is, how do we approach this whole situation? Teshima has the weapons, and I do not believe his threats to be idle ones. If we are to resist his ideas in some way, we have to be extremely cautious."

Lora said, "I know Teshima said that the plans need to remain secret, but I think we need to leak some of this gradually out to the right people, starting with the notion that it is environmentally safe outside the walls. We also need to resist turning over resources for the creation of weapons. All of us here have a better idea about what we have in our divisions than they do. I think we need to conceal things, doctor inventories if necessary, to keep materials out of their hands."

Everyone around the table nodded in agreement. Jonathan said, "Okay. Lora and I can get the environmental info out since that's her field, and I have the most contact with things outside the dome. Let's meet for lunch back here three days from now after we take a look at what each of us can control. We can put together a more definite plan at that time."

The plate lunches were finished in contemplative silence.

***

After seeing Byl and Aaron off, Sam met with Kayli and Nathan back at their *hale*.

"I thought it would be best for the two of you to keep an eye on Hilo Dome, especially since you, Nathan, know more about it than anyone else in our village. However, I think, instead of going through the forest, the two of you should canoe down the coast to an overlook that gives you a clear view of the dome and of the fishing operations in the bay. We especially want to know about any more openings of the dome, to learn what their activities are once they are outside the walls, and to see if fishing operations have changed in any way.

Nathan and Kayli looked at each other and smiled. Finally, a chance to contribute something! Nathan said, "I like that idea, and I think I know the overlook you are talking about. I could see it when I was walking down the beach after I woke up on the shoreline. It does have a perfect view of the bay and Hilo Dome. It shouldn't be too hard to find food there. There's certainly lots of guava and papaya trees, and I think I know where we might be able to catch some *kāhala*."

Sam grinned at that.

Kayli added, "We can take a lot of rice with us in the canoe. Nathan can make a small fire for us to do some cooking now that he has the technique down. Also, we'll have coconut water and milk along with the meat of the nut to eat."

The technique Kayli spoke of was how to start a fire using two pieces of wood and some of the fine fibers from a coconut husk. Using a wild hibiscus tree, Nathan learned how to pare away the bark off one side of the trunk and then to trim a branch down to a dull point. While holding the cut point of the branch at a 30^0 to 45^0 angle against the sliced portion of the trunk and pressing down very firmly while rubbing the pieces of wood together, enough heat was generated to create a small flame on the trunk. The small flame was transferred to the fibers of the inside of the coconut husk, and by blowing on it, a large flame would erupt. Nathan also learned that a coconut could be opened relatively easily by locating the "face" at one end of the nut itself after it was husked. By holding the nut in his hand with the "eyes" up and smacking the top of it very sharply with a rock, the coconut would split open quite neatly along a seam across the top.

"Okay," said Sam, "let's find you two a good canoe, and you can set off tomorrow after you get all your supplies together. Meanwhile, let's make sure you have a big meal tonight with all your favorites since you probably won't be eating all that well down the coast."

Nathan smiled and protested, "Hey! We'll be just fine out there! However, if we can make requests, I'd love some of Mrs. Pahinui's goat skewers tonight."

Sam laughed. "Me, too! Goat it is!"

15
Setting Sail

Just after the sun came up over the ocean, Kayli and Nathan were down at the *halau* where the canoes were stored. Sam had chosen a single-hulled *waʻa kaukahi* for them to use. Built for two people, it was light and fast with an outrigger on the left side for extra stability. There was also plenty of room for them to carry their supplies. They did not need a lot since the initial trip was not far, and they could easily return in less than a day. However, the plan was for them to observe Hilo Dome for several days in a row to get a feel for how often people came out of the structure and specifically to see if they were testing any weapons.

Nathan was very interested to see the *kāhala* operation since that was what his father controlled. At least that was what he did at the time Nathan was swept away by the Wailuku River. His memories of that day were still very clear in his mind, etched by the fear of being pursued by Chief Teshima's men and the power of the river. It had taken him a while to overcome his aversion to water, but once he was comfortable with being out in the ocean, he had become very skilled in handling a *waʻa kaukaki*, either alone or as part of a team.

Their supplies had been gathered the previous night, so it did not take them long to stock the *waʻa kaukaki*. They had lots of cordage made from *olonā* fibers and many long slender poles from the paper mulberry trees that had been lashed next to the hull on the outrigger supports. The cordage and poles were necessary for the construction of a tent-like shelter to protect them from the elements. As Nathan had come to learn, it rained a lot in the area around Hilo. They also packed several pounds of rice, cured meats, dried fruits, woven mats, crossbows, and fishing gear. With Kayli's family watching them from the shore, Kayli and Nathan pushed the outrigger into the gentle waves and hopped in. The surf was not rough as they paddled out and then headed south towards Hilo Dome.

It was actually a short paddle down to their lookout location. In fact, hundreds of years before, this spot was a "Scenic Lookout" giving the viewer a panoramic look out over Hilo Bay and directly into the town itself. Kayli and Nathan nosed the canoe onto the sand, hopped out, and pulled it up beyond the high tide line. After they unloaded their gear, they covered the *waʻa kaukahi* with some palm fronds and other vegetation just in case there were "visitors." Having encountered the two spies from Cook, they knew they had to take precautions.

They found a trail, probably made by wild goats or *puaʻa*, that wound its way up the cliff to the small plateau overlooking the bay. The trail was a good sign; the crossbows might come in handy. When they got to the top with their gear, Nathan said to Kayli, "Okay, it's your choice. You can gather fronds for the shelter covering or you can start lashing the poles together for the framework."

Kayli thought about this for a moment, then said, "It might be easier if we both work on the frame and then gather materials for the covering. Doing it together might be more efficient and safer." Nathan could not argue with that logic, so they set about binding the poles to form a tent-like structure about two meters high and three meters wide.

It took most of the rest of the day to complete their primitive *hale*, pausing only for a quick lunch of papaya and guava they found while collecting the covering material. After rolling out the mats and stowing their gear inside, they made their way back to the canoe and went out for a short paddle around the bay. With only a few hours of daylight left, they did not want to end up trying to find the trail back in the dark.

There was not a whole lot to see. Dominating the shoreline was the main structure of Hilo Dome that covered most of the town and the end of the Wailuku River where Nathan was swept out of the city. Nathan pointed to areas of the dome and explained to Kayli what it was like inside, where his house was, where his mother worked, and how he ended up in the bay. As they paddled toward the dome extension that housed Coconut Island and the fishing operation, they encountered the wooden floats that supported the nets that housed the *kāhala*.

Nathan said, "I'm glad to see the nets out. We might get lucky and be able to catch some decent sized *kāhala*." He then explained how his father directed the operation of the submarines, coordinating their movements to gather up the lines attached to the floats to cinch tight the top of the nets to haul them back.

"At certain low tides when there is a new moon or full moon, the cave-like entrance to the submarine pen and harvest collection area is actually partly exposed. Other than where the Wailuku enters the dome, this is the only area I know of that is open to the outside on a regular basis." They paddled over closer to the island, and Nathan pointed the cave area out to Kayli.

Kayli said, "I've only really seen the harvest operation once when I was fishing here with my family. It seemed to us that the submarines just popped to the surface out of nowhere and then began to circle the enclosure. They also seemed to be extremely powerful; the drag from the nets as they return to the island must be incredible."

Nathan agreed. "My father said they were driven by battery-powered electric motors that generate an enormous amount of torque. Although you typically only see two subs in operation, there are actually four. Two subs are usually undergoing maintenance while the other two are ready to do the work. You can see the solar cells across the top of the dome closest to Coconut Island." He glanced at the setting sun. "We better head back in now."

Kayli and Nathan made their way back to the shoreline at the foot of the cliff, pulled the *waʻa kaukahi* out as they did when they arrived, and again covered it with palm fronds. They went up the path, and Nathan began making a fire. As he worked with the wood, he watched Kayli begin to put together the food they were going to have. Nathan had come to realize that he really enjoyed doing things with Kayli and being able to spend this much time with her, just the two of them, was far better than spying with either Byl or Aaron. He hoped she felt the same way.

Kayli looked over at him. "What would you like with your dried meat and fruit? I can make rice, or I can make rice."

Nathan smiled. "Hmmm, let me think. I guess tonight I'd like the rice."

"Okay, I think I can handle that."

They ate their simple dinner of rice, dried meat, and some of the fresh fruit they had collected earlier in the day. After dinner, they sat together and looked out over the ocean, not saying much, just enjoying being together, then settled in to their primitive *hale* to be well-rested for the following day.

***

While Byl and Aaron made slow but steady progress to the area where they suspected Kawananakoa was setting up operations, Kawananakoa was busy making strategic plans in addition to building canoes. His plan was to launch a two-pronged attack on Hilo Dome, if possible. The obvious point of attack would be by the canoes from the bay, but he still wanted to find a weak spot on the opposite side of the dome. He felt the river was the key. He was reluctant to send out more spies since the ones he was counting on, Michael and Abe, had failed to return, but he did not have a choice if he wanted to execute his attack as planned. He sent two more spies to once again check out the back side of the dome and to then return immediately without any further exploration. His two spies set out on what was an almost collision course with the path of Byl and Aaron.

Kawananakoa, or Kamehameha VI as he liked to think of himself, then returned to directing the boat construction. It had been a slow process. He began to realize his attack flotilla might not be as big as he wanted it to be. However, there was no rush. The dome was not going anywhere.

He had wanted the *waʻa kaukahi* to be large enough for eight warriors. That was not to be. There were no *koa* trees large enough and readily available at the lower elevations, and he did not have the manpower to cut, partially shape, and haul the logs down to Hāʻena. They had wasted a lot of time searching in vain for the large trees. It appeared that four-man canoes would have to do.

Several *waʻa kaukahi* were almost ready, getting the finishing touches before adding the outriggers. Kawananakoa wanted enough to be ready to start training and conditioning his men for the trip around the point to Hilo. They had been on the march for a very long time, and it had been a long time away from the water. Paddling in a synchronous way required a great deal of coordination, and the muscles used for rowing had grown weak from not being used. The first rounds of training should be ready to start in a day or two. Preparations for battle would start in earnest.

16
Everyone Is Learning

Kayli and Nathan spent the next few days exploring their immediate surroundings and observing Hilo Dome. In their explorations, they were looking for trails that might lead to the dome that might enable them to have better cover than they would find on the shoreline if they wanted to move in closer. They were also looking for trees that would provide a good source of fruit or perhaps some nuts. However, guava and papaya seemed to be the only viable options.

On the second day, they made a very nice discovery. Kayli and Nathan came across an abandoned building that appeared to have been an office building or conference center. Like the *hale* they constructed, it had a commanding view of Hilo Bay and had a small black sand beach below it with a protected cove. They carefully explored all the rooms on the first floor but did not risk going upstairs. Kayli explained to Nathan that many of the older buildings in Honoli'i were safe on the first floor, but many of the rooms on second floors did not have flooring that was structurally sound enough to support a person's weight. The last thing they needed was for one of them to get injured.

With the inevitable rain coming, they decided to move their base of operations from the scenic point to the comfort of the huge conference room. They could build cooking fires in the covered portico in the rear of the building and have plenty of room to store equipment and to spread out their mats for sleeping. The view from the building was even better than the scenic point. With protection from the weather, they could keep an eye on the dome even during a downpour.

The observation task was often a boring job since excursions by people outside the dome were few and far between. During the first two days, on several occasions, they saw panels of the dome open up and people in bulky suits come out. They appeared to be getting samples of water and soil, just as Byl and Aaron had witnessed when they captured one of the Cook spies. On the third day, something dramatically different occurred. One of the panels opened, but unlike previous openings, the people that emerged were wearing normal clothing and carrying weapons. One team set up targets and began to shoot at them with crossbows and bows and arrows.

Kayli was not impressed. "It appears that their weapons are either not very good or they are very poor shots, or both." Nathan had to agree. Many of the shots were not even close to the center, and many missed the target altogether. They were impressed by the weapon that used an electric charge, but they could see that it had a very short range of effectiveness. It was hard to see details, so they decided to leave their cliffside perch and move along the shoreline to get a closer look. Taking the *waʻa kaukahi* out into the bay would be far too obvious.

They kept a close watch on the participants of the target practice. It was good that the shooters were totally absorbed in what they were doing. They never even glanced in the direction of the shoreline. After about an hour, one of the men knocked on the side of the dome with his fist, a crack appeared, and one of the panels, about two meters wide and three meters tall, opened outward. Everyone collected their weapons and reentered the dome. The panel closed slowly after them.

Nathan looked at Kayli. "What do you think? It seems to support what Byl and Aaron told us. However, I think we need a closer look at the outside of the dome to see how those panels might work. I never bothered going near the dome wall when I lived inside."

Kayli shook her head. "I'm not sure that's a good idea. What if we are in close and it opens up again? We would almost certainly be spotted, and we really don't want to get in a skirmish with them." She paused for several minutes, trying to think through the idea. Hesitantly, she said, "Okay, but we wait about an hour first to see if anyone else comes out. We can gather limpets for dinner while we wait. We just have to be careful."

"Hey! You know what?" Nathan asked.

"What?"

"We could have rice with them."

"Wow! Great idea!"

Nathan had grown to love eating *opihi* either raw or boiled while living with the Pahinuis. The bay was calm, so it was not at all dangerous to get into the intertidal zone where the limpets lived to do the collecting. Kayli had a *tapa* cloth sack that was half filled when they decided it was safe to move towards the dome exterior. They put the sack in a tide pool to keep the limpets fresh and weighed it down with lava rock so it would not be washed away.

There was a mix of sandal wood and sea grape providing cover as they advanced on the dome. However, when they got within ten meters, it was all open lava rock and weathered concrete. The section of the dome they were facing was opaque, but they could see that, about one hundred meters to their left, it seemed almost transparent, an area obviously to be avoided. They approached cautiously. The ridges between the panels were quite evident, but as Kayli and Nathan navigated the perimeter, they noticed variations in the joints. In most cases, the panels seemed to fit into slots on the edge of the "rib," but in others, the panel seemed to close against a flattened section or flange. These looked like sections that could open. It was nice to be able to thalk in this situation; a whisper here would seem loud enough to be heard inside, or so they thought.

Nathan said, "I think we've seen enough for now." Just as he finished that thought, a loud grinding and creaking noise was heard to their right. The dome was opening. They flattened themselves against the section of the dome they had been inspecting. Luckily, the section that was opening was far enough away that the curvature of the dome prevented them from being seen. It sounded as though just two people were there.

"I told you when we started to do the weapons training that all weapons had to be accounted for. They have to be checked out of our weapons locker, counted as the team reenters, and then checked back into the locker." The tone was quite angry.

"I thought we had them all," said the second person. "Everyone said they had what they came out with."

"Look, you're responsible as team leader. I want your eyes on every weapon with a check off sheet for reentry to the dome. This lapse is inexcusable. We don't have the resources to lose even a single crossbow. Now, where was the firing range? We'll start our search there. There are two crossbows missing according to my records."

Kayli and Nathan were pretty sure they were not in the area of the range, but if the two men could not find the weapons right away, they might stumble upon them in an expanded search. At this point, though, there was nothing for them to do except remain plastered to the dome wall. They could hear the men moving through some vegetation. They were getting closer.

"Hey! Dan! Here they are! Let's get back inside and crank that panel closed. I don't feel very comfortable out here at all!" As the panel could be heard closing, Kayli and Nathan looked at each other and breathed a sigh of relief.

Kayli said, "Okay. Let's get out here, get our bag of *opihi*, and go cook ourselves some dinner."

"Couldn't agree with you more," said Nathan. "Let's talk about expanding our range of surveillance for tomorrow and maybe we could also include a little fishing expedition." Kayli gave Nathan a quizzical look but did not let her thoughts out.

***

Kawananakoa's spies did not have to search for long to discover what might be a potential weakness in the Hilo Dome. They made their way around on the *mauka*, or mountain, side of the dome until they arrived at the waterfall, part of the Wailuku River that sat just outside the dome itself. They worked their way down below the falls to the point where the river actually flowed into the dome. On their march from Cook, they had seen examples of water-powered electrical generators. They had found only two, and they were not very large, but they surmised that the Wailuku was how Hilo was getting its electrical power. If this section of the dome could be sabotaged in some way, it might force the dome to lose power and eventually open the panels after the air handlers shut down. Several large logs rafting down the river just might be enough. They also found several large buildings near the falls that could serve as a base of operations while the logs were being prepared.

They made their way back to Hāʻena and found Kawananakoa down at the beach, supervising the construction of the canoes. When Kawananakoa saw them, he said, "Well, I hope you are bringing me some good news because this construction here has been lagging far behind my expectations."

The spies described what they had seen below the waterfall, and a smile slowly crept across Kawananakoa's face. "This is excellent!" he exclaimed. He instructed the spies to summon his two lieutenants to the beach.

When they arrived, he went over his ideas for the attack. "We should now be able to execute our two-pronged attack on the dome. That is, if the dome opens up after we hit it with logs, and if we ever get enough of these *waʻa kaukahi* built! When the boats are ready and our training is complete, we can divide our forces, sending one large group to the far side of the dome and the other smaller group in *wa'a kaukahi* right into Hilo Bay. We can have the men on the mountain side of the dome attack first and draw their defenses away from the bay. The men in the *wa'a kaukahi* should then be able to land and move into the city without much resistance."

The lieutenants nodded in agreement. Akuma Kuwabara, the largest man in Kawanankoa's small army, liked the sound of this. "Akuma" meant made by the gods of and/or made of Earth, and his appearance matched his name. He was huge and muscular.

He said, "Kawananankoa, I would like to lead the land contingent. I've never been comfortable in any *wa'a kaukahi*." At this point, he glanced meaningfully at the construction taking place close by. "And no offense, but I really don't think I'll be comfortable navigating in one of those."

The other lieutenant, Holokai Bishop, a small wiry man, laughed and said, "That's fine with me, Akuma. I love being on the water. Even my name means being a seafarer." In fact, in canoe races back in Cook, Holokai had never lost, whether paddling alone or with a team.

Kawanankoa said, "Okay, you guys have made it easy for me. We'll have to make several dry runs to see how long it will take us to get our forces to the waterfall and to get our canoes to the entrance of the bay. Timing is of the essence in this attack. Also, the *wa'a kaukahi* will be facing one small difficulty. My spies reported that there is a seawall or breakwater extending across at least two thirds of the entrance to Hilo Bay. We definitely want Hilo's forces engaged on the *mauka* side before our canoes arrive at the restriction on the *makai* side." He looked carefully at each of his trusted lieutenants. "I'm going to leave it up to you to select the men you want to have under your command. I'll give you a day or two to organize this. Then, the training and timing exercises begin!"

***

Unwittingly, the spies had led Byl and Aaron right to their encampment in Hā'ena. Byl and Aaron had stumbled upon them, almost literally, as the spies examined the exterior of the dome where the Wailuku flowed in. If the spies had not been talking so excitedly about their discovery, the two men from Honoli'i might have passed right by them, or worse, run right into them.

Once Byl and Aaron were aware of the spies, they kept themselves at a safe distance and then trailed them back to Hāʻena. When they arrived, they had to be very careful to avoid all the activity surrounding the construction of the *waʻa kaukahi,* which ranged far above Keaʻau all the way down to the beach at Hāʻena. They circumnavigated the old macadamia plantation to the north and crept towards the Hāʻena encampment close to the shoreline. They arrived just in time to hear Kawananakoa describing his plans for the attack on Hilo. This was critical information that they needed to get back to their father in Honoliʻi, but they still needed to assess the troop strength of the attack force.

Byl said to Aaron, "Given the number of completed *waʻa kaukahi,* I think we can spare at least a couple of days to get some accurate numbers. When we passed by the macadamia plantation, there was a large building that may have been where the nuts were processed. We can see if we can spend a few nights there without being discovered by Kawananakoa's men."

Aaron nodded. "That building is so big we can probably build a small fire in there to make some rice, and there are plenty of fruit trees in addition to the macadamia trees. Let's watch the canoe building for a bit more and then move *mauka* to try to count how many workers are bringing logs down from above Keaau. If we repeat that process several times tomorrow, we might only need one more full day on site."

Byl agreed. "I hope Kayli and Nathan are getting some good information from where they are on the bay. From the sound of Kawananakoa's plans, we're going to need some good defensive intervention plans for both side of the dome."

Their attention was suddenly drawn towards the beach by some loud cheering. They were witnessing the celebration of Kawananakoa and his men for the launching of his first four-man *waʻa kaukahi.*

17
The Cave and Beyond

Kayli and Nathan awoke to the early morning sun streaming through the open double doors of the portico. This was so much more comfortable than the small lean-to tent they had constructed, and they were able to keep their fire going for their *opihi* dinner even though a downpour began just after it was started. Although the limpets could be eaten raw, Nathan preferred the boiled preparation, so besides being dry, he also enjoyed his dinner that much more.

They had a breakfast of fresh papaya and began to make plans for their next exploration. Nathan was anxious to check out the *kāhala* pens and the entrance to the underwater cavern that served as the main base of operations for the Hilo aquaculture. He also wanted to paddle out beyond the breakwater and head south along the coast to check out what conditions were like along the shoreline. Their canoe was light and fast; he thought they would be able to cover a great distance in a short period of time. Perhaps they might be able to see where Kawananakoa's naval operations were taking shape. Kayli was not so sure about the last part of the plan, but she decided to let things play out first as they investigated the bay.

One major concern was that when they came into the bay through the breakwater entrance, they would be very visible to anyone standing on the shore outside the dome. So far, all the Hilo activity had been farther inland, and their small *wa'a kaukahi* would not be too obvious. Once they got to Coconut Island, they would be screened by the dome and could operate relatively safely. No matter, it was a chance they would have to take to get good information.

Kayli and Nathan pushed their canoe out into the light chop on the surface of the bay. Typically, Hilo Bay was quite calm, but the portion not protected by the breakwater could, at times, be very rough. They paddled swiftly over to the area where the *kāhala* were located. Nathan wanted to see how big the fish were. Knowing the size of the fish would give him a rough estimate as to when the pen might be pulled into the cave for harvest. Most of the time, there were three pens, each with fish in different stages of growth.

When they arrived at the first pen, they carefully slid their *waʻa kaukahi* through a gap between two of the wooden floats that kept the top of the netting near the surface. Kayli paddled gently, just enough to maintain their position close to the center of the area delineated by the floats. Nathan had already stowed his paddle and had pulled a roasted *kukui* nut out of the small bag he had in the stern of the canoe. Last night, they had been snacking on them, but now they would be put to use in a different way.

Nathan chewed on the nut, but as he had been taught, instead of swallowing, he spit the contents of his mouth out over the surface of the water beside the boat's hull. The oil of the nut released by his chewing created the same effect as if he were wearing polarized sunglasses. The *kukui* nut is also known as the candlenut, so oily that they can be lit, and each nut will burn for about ten to fifteen minutes. The oil reduced the glare on the surface of the water, and Kayli and Nathan could peer down through the oily sheen to get a look at the teeming fish below them.

The fish they could see seemed to be quite large, perhaps as big as four kg. That meant they were almost ready to be harvested. Depending on conditions, the *kāhala* could be harvested between one and a half to two years of age, then sold fresh in the Hilo farmers' market, or frozen for sale over an extended period of time. After they finished their day's explorations, they would stop back at this pen and try their luck at fishing.

When Kayli and Nathan launched their canoe earlier in the morning, they had noticed that it was low tide. In fact, it was an extremely low tide due to the fact that it had been a full moon the previous evening. The tidal shifts around the Hawaiian Islands were not as extreme as in other parts of the world, but Nathan was hoping this tidal shift would be enough to expose the cave-like opening that was the doorway into the cavern that served as the base of operations for the submarines that tended the fish pens.

Coconut Island had been built up centuries ago to support the submarine operation, and the old Hilo Hawaiian Hotel had been converted into a large complex that housed the offices, warehouses, and freezers that supported the aquaculture project that helped to feed the citizens of Hilo Dome. Nathan knew it well; this was where his father, Jonathan Ohana, worked.

Kayli and Nathan paddled out of the pen and headed for the Coconut Island cave entrance. As they approached it, they could see that the top of the arch of the cave entrance was about twenty centimeters above the surface of the water. They tried to peer in, but it was too dark to get a good look at anything. Nathan was pretty sure the entrance was the beginning of a tunnel that did not open up until it was squarely under the island. The dome here came almost to the water's edge. It was opaque and reinforced to withstand any wave action that might occur when storms swept in from the ocean. Big storm waves could totally submerge the breakwater. In fact, the old museum in Hilo had information about tsunamis that ravaged the town well before the dome was built, with waves sweeping water several blocks into the town center. Nathan was disappointed that he could not get a better look into the tunnel, and he was not sure knowing the cave was partially exposed at low tide would prove to be useful.

Nathan sighed, "Well, Kayli, I don't think we're going to discover much more right in this area. We can either go back to observing the dome, or we can do a little more exploration while we are out in our *wa'a kaukahi*. I think we should take a look down the coast outside the breakwater. I know you were hesitant about the idea last night, but it doesn't seem too dangerous out here right now."

Kayli nodded. "Okay, but just for a little while. I do want to come back here and do a little fishing before the sun sets. We need something to go with the rice."

"Haha!"

They paddled out through the breakwater, turned right, and headed east down the coast. They stayed close to the shoreline and were astonished to find beautiful beaches and secluded coves. They could also see many old buildings, abandoned long ago and totally overgrown with vegetation. Apparently, no human had been in this area for a very long time. They paddled into a small cove and saw about twenty *honu* resting on the sun-drenched beach. They were tempted to come ashore, but Kayli convinced Nathan that the risk was too great.

They finally arrived at a point where the coastline made a radical turn and headed south. As much as Nathan wanted to continue farther, it was getting late, and there were some fish that were just waiting to be caught and turned into a delicious meal. So, they came about and headed back to Hilo Bay.

As they paddled past the cove, Nathan said, "C'mon! Let's go ashore and check these turtles out. They are the biggest *honu* I've ever seen. Maybe this is a breeding area."

Kayli sighed and said, "OK, but just for a short time. We still have fish to catch, remember?"

They turned the *wa'a kaukahi* towards the shore and minutes later made a soft landing on the beach. They clambered out of the canoe into warm water that was not quite up to their knees and hauled the canoe up on the beach so that just the stern was in the water.

Kayli and Nathan walked along the shoreline keeping a safe distance between themselves and the turtles so as not to disturb them. Nathan explained that he had read that, at one point of Hawaii's history, it was against the law to disturb these huge beasts. The *honu*, for their part, seemed totally oblivious to their presence.

As they were approaching what looked like the largest one, Kayli stopped abruptly, so abruptly that Nathan, who was walking right behind her, bumped into her. Kayli seemed not to even notice the collision; she was staring down at her feet. Nathan followed the path of her vision and gave out a slight gasp. Kayli said, "Nathan, I don't think we're alone here."

18
The Village

Kayli and Nathan bent down to look at the footprints they had just stumbled upon. The first thing they noticed was the size; the prints were all small, considerably smaller than even Kayli's. There were many of them, scattered all around the *honu*, but then it seemed as though they converged together and moved up the beach towards the line of tall Australian pines that lined the upper reaches of the beach all around the cove. They followed the trail in the sand and discovered a path through some dense vegetation that was just behind the pines.

At this point, they stopped, looked at each other, and then looked back to the path. Kayli said, "What do you think we should do? They seem to be the footprints of children."

"Or very tiny people."

Kayli gave Nathan a "look." "Right. Or very tiny people. Let's assume they are children. How many do you figure were here?" They went back to where they first found them near the turtles, then moved carefully back to the start of the path.

Nathan said, "Just a guess, but I'd say five or six?" It was more of a question than a statement, but Kayli agreed. "What now? Shall we VERY carefully follow the path to see where it leads?"

"I don't know, Nathan. Part of me says, 'Yes, let's do that,' while another part of me wants to jump back in the *wa'a kaukahi* and get out of here as fast as we can. The only thing that makes me feel at all safe is the fact that they are kids' prints. I doubt that this has anything to do with Kawananakoa's army. I'm sure they don't have children tagging along."

"Okay, let's move very slowly and try to pick up any signs of conversation." Nathan stepped off the beach and onto the path. It was just wide enough for the two of them to walk side-by-side, which indicated this more than just a path made by *pua'a* or wild goats; people used this path on a regular basis.

After fifteen minutes, Nathan suddenly came to a halt. They had been moving so carefully that they had only traversed about fifty meters of the trail. The path had curved slightly, and the vegetation was so thick they could no longer see the beach, which was a bit unnerving.

Nathan said, "I'm sensing something. Multiple conversations or something like that."

Kayli nodded. "Me, too. Let's move along a little farther to see if it gets clearer. If we are at the edge of our thalk perception, there could still be another one hundred meters between us and whoever is talking."

As they moved slowly along the path, the conversations did become more distinct, but they were hard to break down since there seemed to be many being held simultaneously. They both came to the conclusion that there was a lot of human activity ahead. Kayli looked up into the forest canopy. "From what I'm seeing, there appears to be some sort of clearing not too far in the distance. I'm thinking we should get off this path and try to work our way through the vegetation."

Nathan agreed, and they stepped off the path into an area of young *'ōhi'a lehua* and guava trees, ginger plants, *hāpu'u* tree ferns and nasturtium. It was relatively easy to move through, and at the same time, provided a great deal of cover. Soon, the clearing Kayli detected became more obvious. In the clearing was something they were not expecting at all: a village!

Nestled into a broad clearing about one hundred meters in diameter were two decrepit old houses surrounded by a dozen thatched *hale*. It looked like a much smaller, much more dilapidated version of Honoli'i. About a dozen naked children were running around an open space in the village playing what looked like some kind of game of tag. Trying to ignore them were three older women sitting on a bench. As Kayli and Nathan watched, a much older woman with gray hair approached them carrying three dead chickens by their feet. She handed one to each woman and said, "Okay, let's get these ready for tonight's dinner." It was obvious where the chickens were heading. In the center of the opening were two small fire pits, each containing a spit and lined with lava rock.

Across the village and in front of one of the thatched *hale*, two men were repairing a cast net for fishing while another sat nearby making what appeared to be fishing line. From their conversation, Kayli and Nathan learned they planned to go fishing early the next morning. Several spears leaned against the front of the *hale*. Whether they were for hunting, spearing octopus, or for defense, Kayli and Nathan could only guess.

All the adults were clothed in simple wraps made of *kapa* cloth around their waists. Both the men and women wore a variety of necklaces; most of the women's were *kukui* nut while the men seemed to prefer shark's teeth.

Unlike Honoli'i, there was virtually no sign of agriculture, other than a large stand of banana trees at the far side of the village and two goats tethered outside one of the *hale*. As Kayli and Nathan watched, the women yelled to the children, directing the oldest of the group to go harvest some bananas. Upon hearing this, the youngest ones laughed and screamed and ran off down another path leading out of the village. Nathan said, "I guess they have their freedom for the day."

As Kayli and Nathan watched, they came to the conclusion that this group of people was very isolated from everything else and operated primarily as hunter-gatherers with just a minimal amount of agriculture to stabilize their diets. Totally fascinated observing daily life in this primitive village, they were both startled as they heard the group of younger children come running down the path behind them. They crouched down in the vegetation as the children passed.

"Mama! Papa! There's something on the beach! Something's on the beach!" They ran up to their parents, jabbering away. Kayli and Nathan knew what was on the beach—their *wa'a kaukahi*! While confusion reigned as the kids yelled and the parents tried to figure out what was actually going on, Kayli and Nathan backed away from their observation area, then turned and sprinted down the path to the beach.

They did not look back until they reached the canoe. They pushed it out into deeper water, clambered in, grabbed their paddles, and quickly got the *wa'a kaukahi* underway. Finally, well away from the shoreline, they looked back to see three men carrying spears emerge from where the path broke through the Australian pines. The men continued to stare after them until they rounded the next point of land heading back to Hilo. Only then did they slow their pace and breathe a sigh of relief.

"Okay, that was WAY too close!" Kayli exclaimed.

"You can say that again," said Nathan.

"Okay, that was way—"

"Stop!"

They both laughed as the tension eased away. They resumed their trek towards the fishing pens in a much more leisurely way.

Nathan was puzzled by one thing during the encounter. Is it possible that the villagers did not even have canoes? The children kept saying there's "something" on the beach. They did not say "boat" or "canoe" or "*waʻa kaukahi.*" Also, the men were repairing a cast net, one that is used from the shoreline or standing in shallow water. He shared this idea with Kayli, who tended to agree with his conclusion.

"I can see one problem they may be facing as a far as a canoe is concerned," Kayli said. "There are no trees on this section of the island that are big enough."

"We'll definitely have to describe this as accurately as possible to your dad to see what he thinks. It's interesting that there can be people in so many stages of development in this relatively small area of the island."

Kayli agreed. "Well, the dome is a huge barrier between our village and theirs. And until we became aware of Kawananakoa, we were not even sure there were other people, "Ferals" as they are known in Hilo Dome, still alive on this island at all."

Nathan thought about this for a few moments. "It's really interesting, and when and if this whole thing developing with Hilo Dome, Kawananakoa, and us gets resolved, I would love to do some serious island exploration."

Kayli looked at Nathan. "I'd be glad to be part of that exploration team. But for now, let's get back to Hilo Bay and the *kāhala* pens!"

They positioned themselves in the center of the pen where they had seen the large *kāhala* earlier in the day. Kayli and Nathan each had a fishing line with a bone hook attached to one end. They secured bits of dried meat on the hooks and lowered them by hand over the side of the hull.

Nathan said, "Well, I hope this doesn't take too lon—" Before he could finish his sentence, he felt a sharp tug on his line. "Wow! I think I've hooked one already!" As he pulled his line in, he could see that Kayli was doing the same. Within minutes, there were two large *kāhala* flopping around in the bottom of the boat.

Nathan said, "I guess they were really tired of eating those soy and bone meal pellets the subs spray into the pens."

Kayli agreed. "Dad said this would be easy, but I didn't think it would be this easy!"

The fish were no longer so enthusiastic in their flopping, so Kayli fashioned a stringer out of another piece of line, threaded it through the mouth and gill of each fish, and handed them to Nathan, who lowered them gently into the water over the stern of the boat. "That should keep them fresh until we get back."

They paddled slowly back to their shelter, keeping an eye on the dome, but no panels opened up, and no one was outside. Kayli said, "I guess we'll give it another day or two. Then, we'd better get back to Honoli'i. If there's no word from Byl and Aaron, we can always come back."

Nathan agreed. "Now, let's go clean and cook some fish!"

***

Kayli and Nathan sat under the portico after dinner, watching the moon creep up over the horizon. It still looked as big and full as it did the night before.

"You know, I never thought I would want to eat another piece of *kāhala* again. That's all we ever ate back when I was in the dome, that and chicken."

Kayli laughed. "Yeah, I remember you saying that a lot when you first arrived in our village. I just used my mom's cooking techniques. I'm really glad you liked it."

"Well, you obviously learned from the best." They sat staring at the moon for a few moments, then Nathan said, "You know, back when we made our escape from the village and we were heading back to the *kāhala* pen, I said I'd like to explore the island when things settle down and you said you'd like to be part of my exploration team."

Kayli nodded.

"Did you really mean that? I mean, there's no one I'd rather have along with me than you."

Kayli looked at Nathan, slid a little closer to him, and put her head on his shoulder. "Yes, of course I really meant it. I think it would be great to be with you on adventures around the island."

She picked her head up and looked right into Nathan's eyes. "You might be stuck with me for a long time!"

Kayli put her head back on Nathan's shoulder, and they watched the moon as it continued to rise over the calm water.

19
Building the Fleet

Byl and Aaron continued their observations for several days, using the former macadamia nut factory as their base. The rate at which Kawananakoa was able to build his fleet was increasing. Most of the raw materials were now on site, so it now became a matter of fully hollowing out the *koa* logs and constructing and affixing the outriggers to the hulls. With most of the activity now in the Hāʻena region, it was also easier for Byl and Aaron to get an idea as to how many men were part of Kawananakoa's army.

With ten *waʻa kaukahi* completed, Kawananakoa was able to send men out into the ocean in shifts to train together. After two or three hours of maneuvers, they would come ashore and rotate with the crews who were constructing the canoes. Over the course of a day, most of the men would cycle through canoe training, canoe building, and hunting for and gathering food. Byl and Aaron estimated the total number of men to be just over three hundred, a considerable force given that Hilo, at this time, just had a small police force with very few weapons, and they had no presence out in the water whatsoever.

From what they could see, Byl and Aaron estimated that perhaps thirty *waʻa kaukahi* would be completed. With four men in each canoe, that meant that the number of men arriving through Hilo Bay would be around one hundred and twenty. With the initial invasion occurring on the *mauka* side of the dome, these men could easily sweep through the city, taking hostages and occupying buildings.

It was time to get back to Honoliʻi to share their information and formulate a course of action for their village to take. It was obvious that Hilo was in dire straits and had no idea what to expect in terms of a Kawananakoa siege.

***

After establishing that Hilo Dome was holding limited weapons training on a daily basis, Kayli and Nathan returned to Honoliʻi. Sam was very interested to hear what they had discovered. However, it would be difficult to draw up plans of action until Byl and Aaron completed the picture. He was not sure if Hilo was a threat to them, or if Kawananakoa was a threat to them, or both. From Kayli and Nathan's observations, it was likely that Hilo Dome considered Honoli'i to be a threat since they had no idea that an army from Cook was almost at their doorstep.

Sam was not really surprised to learn about the village on the other side of the dome. He had assumed that since the town of Cook existed, there had to be others out there. However, he was surprised to learn that the village was so small and operating primarily as a hunter-gatherer tribe. What a shock it would be to them if they encountered the army from Cook! At least now they were aware that there were other people living outside the dome thanks to Kayli and Nathan's impromptu visit.

After the debriefing session was completed, Sam said, "Well, I guess you two are expecting another feast now that you've returned."

Kayli and Nathan looked at each other and shook their heads. Kayli said, "That's not necessary. We actually ate pretty well while we were gone. We had plenty of fish, thanks to Nathan's dad, *opihi*, and even octopus one night. The building we discovered was a perfect place to live and served beautifully as a place to observe the dome."

"I'm glad we didn't have to stay in the shelter we constructed for the first night," Nathan added. "We had some overnight downpours that would have gone right through it. We're going to have to get a lot better at that skill if we're going to explore the rest of the island."

Sam looked at each of them in surprise. "Explore the rest of the island? Where did that idea come from?"

Kayli said, "Well, after we discovered the small village, we thought it would be interesting, once this whole problem with Hilo Dome and Kawananakoa is resolved, to really see what's out there, how people are living, and just how they've adapted to their surroundings. I'm actually kind of surprised we haven't done more of that."

Sam was nodding as she said all this. "It is something we thought about, but we were always trying to balance the pros and cons of doing something like that. As we can see from the people from Cook, there can be some real dangers. But it might be time to start making connections with other groups and sharing some of our success in establishing a community." He paused, giving it some more thought. "I think it's a good idea, but first things first; let's get this brewing conflict resolved."

Kayli and Nathan volunteered to do some fishing to get something for dinner while Sam went to meet with members of the town council to let them know that Kayli and Nathan were back safely and had lots of good information for them to consider.

***

As planned, after three days had passed, Lora, Jonathan, and other town leaders met once more at the L & L. Everyone was a bit more relaxed this time, having had the chance to review what their divisions might be able to do to get through this situation.

As expected, no one was anxious to give up resources or personnel to fuel the war-like aspirations of Mayor Hapuna and Chief Teshima. However, the two men still had the police force and weapons on their side, so caution would be necessary.

Everyone at the table described similar reactions when they shared the idea of opening the dome with a few select others. Without being privy to the information that it might be environmentally safe outside the dome, the news of opening the panels was met with shock and horror. After all, many still believed that there were radioactive monsters roaming the mountainsides. Even when it was explained to them that it would be safe, there was a great deal of doubt. An enclosed dome was all they had ever known.

No one was in favor of initiating an attack on other people without further exploration. Most were aware of the "Ferals," but most had also assumed that they would be peaceful people. They certainly would not have the technology that was available to the citizens of Hilo Dome. Also, no one was in favor of conscription into a militia.

Mayor Hapuna had announced a town meeting was to be held in two days. Jonathan said he expected the mayor to announce the draft idea at that time.

Jonathan said, "I think we should be prepared to protest this decision as a group. Go back to the people you spoke with already and see if they would be willing to speak up at this meeting if the opportunity presents itself. If Hapuna pushes this forward without the consent of our citizens, we may have to consider other options."

***

Two days after Kayli and Nathan arrived back home, Byl and Aaron returned. Sam gathered the four of them together to hear about what Byl and Aaron saw and to compare notes. It would then be time to develop a strategy.

Byl and Aaron explained what was happening in Hāʻena and what Kawananakoa was planning to do. They also described how many men they saw and how the workday was divided into shifts. They estimated that about an additional twenty *waʻa kaukahi* would be completed in just a few days and that a few more days of training would follow. After that, they believed Kawananakoa could attack Hilo Dome at any time.

Sam agreed. "I think you are right that this army plans to attack the dome rather than our village. However, if they are successful, we'll be next in line. So, what can we do to thwart their attempts to take over Hilo?"

Aaron said, "Their point of attack will be to disrupt the power being generated by the Wailuku River as it flows through the dome. Is there some way for us to prevent that from happening?"

Kayli was slowly shaking her head. "I'm concerned that they will have too many men in that area for us to safely intervene there. From what you have said, they'll have around two hundred trained fighters there. I don't think we can generate enough numbers from our village to confront them, and even if we did, a direct confrontation would result in heavy losses on both sides."

Nathan said, "I agree with Kayli. Their weaponry is similar to ours, and we don't really know exactly when they plan to initiate their attack. We could be there for weeks waiting for them to come. It would be hard for us to muster up a large army and then be able to maintain its presence there for an extended period of time."

Everyone was quiet for a few minutes, but then Sam spoke up. "I think we may have to leave Hilo Dome on its own when it comes to defending the *mauka* side of their enclosure. That doesn't mean we can't help them in some way. I'm thinking we can warn them somehow, but I'm concerned that getting their attention and then trying to communicate effectively would be problematic. They probably already think we were responsible for the man that was shot by the Cook spies."

Byl said, "Maybe the first thing we should do is post a couple of people near the Wailuku entrance on a rotating basis. We need to have some kind of heads-up for when they might begin the attack. It wouldn't be that big of a commitment, and it's something we can easily manage."

Sam said, "Not a bad idea for starters." He smiled at Byl. "I guess since it's your idea, you can organize it."

Byl responded with a sarcastic, "Thanks, Dad!" After getting some chuckles out of the group, he quickly added, "Yeah, no problem. We know plenty of people who would commit to this."

Sam said, "That's one small step, but how do we warn the people of the dome that an attack is eminent so that they can be prepared? On top of that, we haven't addressed how the dome will respond to a two-pronged attack. They may not have the resources to handle even the *mauka* attack let alone a surprise invasion coming off the bay."

They sat in silence for a while before Nathan spoke up. "I think I might have a solution for both of those problems, but it's a little risky—for me." Upon hearing this, Kayli reached out and grasped Nathan's hand, which drew the attention of her father. He said nothing, though.

"Okay, Nathan. What's the plan?" Sam asked.

"When Kayli and I were doing our observations, we got an up-close view of the submarine entrance into Coconut Island. It was a full moon and low tide, and the top of the entrance was partially exposed. On the next new moon, or perhaps the following full moon, I think I could get into the dome by swimming on my back through the tunnel. There should be enough space for me to keep my mouth and nose exposed so I can breathe."

Aaron interrupted, "Um, Nathan, that sounds crazy, but do go on."

"Once I get inside, I would make my way to my parents' house and tell them what we know. I think once they understand what is at stake, they will be able to convince the mayor and the chief that they all face imminent danger."

Sam was nodding his head while at the same time looking very doubtful. "Okay, so let's say you are successful in reaching your parents AND they are able to convince the authorities that Kawananakoa is about to attack; how do they handle the dual-sided attack? Do you think they have the ability to fend off invaders at both sides of the dome simultaneously?"

Kayli shook her head. "Not from what we saw. Their weapons training seems to be moving very slowly, and it hasn't involved many people. Those electric pistols will be effective in close quarters, but how long will they operate without a recharge? I think it will be difficult for them to avoid being overrun from just the *mauka* attack, let alone a two-sided invasion."

Byl said, "I think once the Kawananakoa army is engaged on the *mauka* side, we should be able to successfully attack them from the rear and pin them down between us and the dome. We would be attacking from above, giving us an advantage. We would also have the element of surprise."

"Okay, I think we can do that effectively and still keep our people safe," Sam said, "However, that's about all we can do. We do not have enough people to do a pincer attack from both the *mauka* side and the *makai* side attack from the bay. We would be spread too thin."

"That's where my father comes in!" Everyone turned to look at Nathan, and he looked back at Sam. "Remember when you told me the story about the baby in the boat?" Sam nodded. "You said that the submarine hit the *waʻa kaukahi*, shearing off the outrigger and capsizing the canoe. I'm betting that my father can have three—if not all four—of the subs ready to move out into the bay when the attack starts. According to Byl and Aaron, the *mauka* attack will begin first. That should give my father time to mobilize the submarines before Kawananakoa's canoes can enter the bay through the breakwater."

Aaron asked, "Okay, then what does he do? Have them roam around blindly hoping to disrupt enough canoes to do significant damage?"

Nathan said, "Look, you've been in the bay. That breakwater has a relatively narrow entrance. If the subs maneuvered back and forth on both sides of the entrance, it would create, at the very least, an effective blockade to prevent an attack. Plus, I think we can do more than that. I think we can capsize most of their *waʻa kaukahi* fleet."

"It's a good idea," Sam said. "But how are the subs guided? Your father's control area is underground. It's not like he can see where Kawananakoa's boats are. I know he has some control over the subs since they tend to the pens and harvest the fish, but I assumed that was all pretty automated."

"For the most part, it is," Nathan agreed. "However, they can act independently apart from the automation. He has screens that can track each sub as a different colored blip as they move around the bay, and he can control each one independently."

"That's a lot to control at one time," said Kayli. "How will he do that?"

"He has lots of help controlling the subs for feeding and harvest. Many of the people who work for him are capable of doing the operations even if he isn't there, although that's a very rare occurrence. Plus, I think we can help him find where the *waʻa kaukahi* actually are out in the bay."

Sam looked puzzled. "How will we do that?"

"We'll have a spotter feeding me information, and I'll be beside my father signing to him about the canoe locations or pointing them out on the screen. I'm sure our thalk capabilities will work fine if someone is positioned right above the control area. It's got some elevation and has a good view over the whole bay."

"And who will this 'spotter' be?"

"Kayli and I have been a good team so far. I think she would make an excellent spotter!"

Sam looked at Kayli. "Well, Kayli, what do you think?"

"I think it is something I could definitely do. Nathan and I do work well together."

Sam stood up, signaling that the meeting was over for now. "I would like all of you to really think about what we have just discussed and see if it is something you think we can actually do. I'm going to go see Edward Park and a few others to get their opinions as well. Then, we can meet to see if this is really feasible, and if it is, to finalize the plans."

***

They gathered again the following day. Over the course of the evening, Sam met with members of the village council and also heard from Nathan and Byl. They had some modifications they wanted to discuss with the group.

Sam said, "I think we'll start with Byl. And then hear from Nathan. They have the most critical changes to make to the plans we discussed yesterday. Byl, you have the floor."

"Aaron and I were discussing what we suggested yesterday and realized that having someone keep watch near the Wailuku just outside the dome would not give Nathan enough lead time to get inside and warn his father about the impending attack. We are now going to suggest that we take up a watch in Hāʻena where

Aaron and I gathered our information. The old macadamia nut factory is a relatively safe haven, and we won't need to get too close to simply assess the status of Kawananakoa's operations. Two people would be able to easily outrun a mobilized army and get back here within a day. It will take at least two days for an army to move from Hā'ena to Hilo Dome and then probably another day for their attack preparations, perhaps a little more."

"I think that's a pretty accurate assessment, Byl." Sam paused to see if others had anything to say. "Have you formulated a watch rotation so that the same people are not stuck out there for an extended period of time?"

"Yes, I think we have a good plan. I'm going to go first along with someone who has not been there before. Three days after we leave, Aaron will follow with another new person. Three days after that, the person I took on the first round will take another new person. With this kind of rotation, there is a smooth turnover of information, and there will always be someone in place who has been there before."

As he spoke, everyone in the group was nodding in agreement. Sam asked Byl, "Anything else we need to consider?"

"Yeah, one more thing. How will we let Nathan know when the attack is about to begin? If he's in the dome, we won't be able to get word to him. Our thalk capabilities don't reach far enough."

Nathan spoke up, "That's what I was going to bring up in terms of modifying my part of the plan. I think I'm going to have to make two trips. The first will be to warn my father. I'm sure he will need some time to try to get three, and perhaps all four, of the subs ready. He will also have to decide how he's going to let the rest of the dome know how he got this warning, especially the mayor and chief. Plans this complex don't come about simply by an intuitive guess. I certainly don't know how he will do that, but I'm going to leave that up to him and my mother."

Kayli added, "We were discussing this problem last night. Mayor Hapuna and Chief Teshima may view this as a trick, especially if they learn the warning came from Nathan, the very person they drove out of the dome."

"Well, the most important thing is to warn my father so he can get the subs ready. How they deal with the rest of the dome will be in their hands. I plan to make this first trip a short one. Our house is not far from the submarine base, and I should be in and out of there in just a couple of hours. Kayli is going to come with me as far as the cave entrance, and then she will stand watch over the *wa'a kaukahi* while I'm inside. We'll come back to Honoliʻi as quickly as possible and then await news from Byl and Aaron's watch teams."

"I'm not sure I like the idea of you having to make two trips in and out of the dome," Sam said.

"I really don't see any other way around it. The most serious problem I face will be hitting the tides correctly so I can breathe as I go through the cave to get to the cavern that holds the subs. I'm not sure how long it is. If it is short, for the second trip, I may be able to hold my breath long enough so that we aren't dependent on the tidal cycle. I'm assuming Kawananakoa couldn't care less about the tides when it comes to launching his attack."

Aaron said, "Well, I could see it working both ways as far as the tides are concerned. It's not the tides themselves he might be considering. It might be visibility. A new moon would provide some darkness so his men could remain concealed during a nighttime attack. If he's not concerned about concealment but needs some visibility to set up the attack, he might choose a full moon. I think it's likely to be one or the other."

Sam looked at Nathan. "I have to agree with Aaron's assessment. I'm assuming you would like to do the first visit sooner rather than later. There's a new moon coming up in just over a week; I think we should get you ready to go then. Byl and Aaron, get your teams ready to start their cycles in a couple of days. From what Byl and Aaron discovered, we still have some time, but once Kawananakoa sets things in motion, things will be changing very quickly."

"You're right, Sam, I'd like to try to get into the dome on the next new moon."

Kayli said, "Do you think you'll need a disguise? Maybe we should at least find a way to dye your hair."

"I'll be going in at night, so I don't think anyone will notice me. However, on the second trip, I may be staying for an extended period of time. I'll probably be able to stay in my parents' house the whole time. If I have to go over to the submarine base, I'll go at night with my dad."

Sam looked around at everyone. "*Mahalo* for getting these plans together so quickly. I think we have our work cut out for us, but it is the best we can do right now. I'm going to start rounding up volunteers for the group that will be attacking Kawananakoa's army from the rear. I don't think I'll have a problem with that." Sam stood up and looked each person in the eye.

"*Mahalo* to each and every one of you."

***

After the meeting, Kayli and Nathan took a walk on the beach. Kayli took Nathan's hand as they walked. "I guess you're worried about doing this. I mean, you don't show it, but you must have some concerns about returning to the dome after so many years."

"You've got that right!" Nathan stopped and looked at her. "What if my parents are no longer doing the same jobs as they were doing when I left? Maybe what I did cost them in some way. My biggest fear is that one or both of them is dead."

Kayli let go of Nathan's hand and threw her arms around him, giving him a big hug. "I wish I could tell you they are both fine and that they still have their jobs. I can't. All I can do is tell you that I *believe* everything is fine and that there will be a very tearful reunion. I wish I could be there to see that."

"Well, when this is all over, you'll get to meet them, and they'll get to meet all of your family. I'm sure they'll want to thank you all for taking such good care of me and for making me a welcome part of your village."

"It's not *my* village, Nathan. It's *our* village."

"Okay, it's *our* village." Nathan smiled.

"What's the smile for?" Kayli asked.

"Oh, just trying to imagine the culture shock on both sides when we all get to meet. Maybe we should have a big *luau,* and my parents and the others from Hilo Dome can get to try some of the great food they've been missing out on all their lives."

"You know," Kayli said, "sometimes, I think food is all you think about."

"No, no, no, you have that wrong." Nathan paused. "Every once in a while, just every once in a while, I think about you."

Kayli let go of Nathan and gave him a quick jab in the arm. "Okay, okay! I think about you just as much as I think about food."

Kayli gave him a sharp frown, turned, and started down the beach, heading back to the town. Nathan quickly ran after her and put his arm around her. "Okay, I admit it. I think about you *way* more than food."

Kayli turned towards him, threw her arms around him again, and said, "There. Was admitting that so hard?" She gave him a quick kiss, and he kissed her back.

"No, that was really nice," Nathan said. "But I guess we should get back soon; it's almost time for dinner."

Kayli sighed, loosened her hug a bit, and gave Nathan an exasperated look. She took his hand again and started back to town. "Always the romantic."

"Yeah, that's me, all right!"

20
Home Sweet Home

A week had passed since Sam Pahinui had gathered everyone together for the planning meeting. Byl and Jeffrey Park, Edward Park's son, had already left for the first round of observations at Kawananakoa's base, and Aaron and one of his friends were to depart the next day to relieve them from their watch. Also leaving the next day were Kayli and Nathan. They were going to return to their building that overlooked Hilo Bay to await the best conditions for Nathan to make his attempt to return to his home. A day or two before or after the new moon would work, as long as the water was relatively calm in the bay. It did not appear that the weather would be uncooperative.

Kayli and Nathan had a quiet dinner with the Pahinui family and awoke the next morning to a breakfast of papaya and some guava juice. They packed their light, two-person *waʻa kaukahi* with the same provisions as before, but this time they did not need the materials to build a shelter. The building they discovered and stayed in on the previous trip was more than adequate to meet their needs.

After they arrived, they unpacked the canoe and took everything up to the building. Then, they decided to see if there had been any changes to the drills that had been taking place outside the dome. They dropped down to the shoreline and made their way closer to the dome. After about an hour, a panel on the dome opened, and a group of men came out carrying a variety of weapons. Kayli and Nathan watched them for a while and quickly decided that either this was a new group or there had been no improvement in weapons handling during the time they were gone.

Kayli said to Nathan, "Let's head over to the cave entrance to see how we can make the best approach when I drop you off. I'll need to have a safe area to pull the *waʻa kaukahi* up to wait for you to come back out."

"Good idea," Nathan replied. "We have plenty of time before sunset. Let's take some fishing gear too."

They carefully left their observation position and returned to their canoe located at the base of the cliff where their shelter was located. Nathan went up to the building and got some dried meat for bait. After he returned, they slid the *waʻa kaukahi* into the water and headed for Coconut Island.

When they arrived at the island, they could see the top of the cave entrance, but just barely. They would have to monitor the tides so that they would be able to enter the cave at night with enough airspace for Nathan to breathe. It looked as though he could make an attempt in the next day or two.

Coconut Island itself was actually outside the dome. Technically, it was not an island anymore. The peninsula called Coconut Island had lost the "island" status many years ago. When the cavern was excavated, the top was reinforced with the lava rock that had once been inside the cavern, and the small channel that was between the island and Hilo was filled in. Over the years, plants eventually took over the bare rock. It was now covered with the vegetation that lined most of Hilo Bay. It would be easy for Kayli to stay out of sight even in broad daylight, if necessary.

As they paddled around Coconut Island, they discovered a small cove on the south side of the peninsula, a perfect spot to come ashore. A very small, coarse sandy beach had formed, out of sight of the office building where Nathan's father worked.

"This will be just fine for me," said Kayli. "After I drop you off, I can pull in here and climb up on the mound. With this vegetation here, I won't be spotted."

Nathan agreed that it was the ideal spot, so they went over to the fish pen to try their luck. As before, it did not take long until they had all they needed.

***

Two days after scouting the island for a landing site and having monitored the tidal cycle in the bay, Nathan was ready to give entering the cave a try. They estimated the lowest point of the cycle to be a few hours after sunset. This worked out well since most of the inhabitants of Hilo would be in their houses after having eaten dinner, and there should be no one in the cavern housing the submarines. No guards were needed in the small, confined city of Hilo.

After eating a light supper, Kayli and Nathan made their way down the path on the cliff face. It took longer than usual since there was no moon visible in the sky and the path was steep. They slid the *waʻa kaukahi* into the water and paddled quietly across the bay to the cave entrance.

Nathan was wearing just his shorts but had taken the precaution of strapping a knife to his calf encased in a sheath of pigskin. He had no intention of using it, but he felt safer just knowing he had at least some defense if he was spotted and cornered. He was more concerned about how his parents would react. It was something that had been troubling him for days. He certainly did not want to frighten his parents; he had changed so much since he was swept away, they might not even recognize him.

Nathan sat towards the bow of the *waʻa kaukahi* since it would be easier for Kayli to pilot the boat from the stern after he got in the water. In the dim light, he could just barely make out the silhouette of the dome, but that was all he needed to direct Kayli to the cave entrance. When they arrived at the entrance, Nathan took several deep breaths to steady his nerves and then silently slipped into the water over the port side of the canoe. Hanging on to the hull, he worked his way back to Kayli.

Taking her hand in his he said, "You'll be okay, right?"

Trying to keep her voice steady, Kayli said, "It's you I'm worried about. I'll be just fine. Please, please be careful!"

"I will." With that, Nathan swam off towards the entrance.

The bay was virtually flat, and for that, Nathan was extremely grateful. He found the entrance quite easily, but then it was time for the totally unknown part. He flipped on to his back and was able to reach out and touch the ceiling of the cave with one hand. There was about thirty centimeters of clearance, plenty of room for breathing, for now. He had no idea how wide the cave was below him or if the ceiling would be the same height all the way through, but he did know about how big the subs were that made the transit through here. As long as he stayed centered on the arch over him, he should not hit any obstructions.

Nathan began a very gentle frog kick, and by having his hand lightly brush against the ceiling, he could determine that he was making slow but steady progress. If he stopped kicking, he could tell that there was a very light current working against him, probably coming from the small stream that emptied out of the pond in Liliʻuokalani Park just inside the dome. It was not strong enough to have an impact on his progress; it just made the water a little colder than the open bay.

After what seemed like an hour but was just a little more than five minutes, he could no longer touch the ceiling, and a dim glow revealed the huge cavern. He flipped over on his stomach and stayed absolutely still for a few minutes. He was at the edge of a very large pool perhaps one hundred meters wide. He could also see two submarines moored to his left and another two moored to his right. Where a conning tower would be on a manned submarine sat a large dorsal fin making the sub appear to be the world's largest shark. He knew there were two sets of fins below the water on each side of the boat. One of each pair was a stabilizer, and the other could rotate to make the sub dive or surface, as needed.

He did a slow breaststroke over to his left after he determined no one was in the cavern. He was very gradually getting used to the dim light provided by what he assumed to be emergency lights. Eventually, he located a ladder just past the stern of the second sub that enabled him to clamber up on a walkway. Nathan turned right and, staying close to the wall, made his way slowly to what he hoped would be an unlocked door. He figured it would be locked for someone trying to exit the cavern, but he might have to find a way to keep the door from locking behind him.

Nathan reached the door. It had a simple push-bar opener, so he assumed it would probably lock behind him. In a trash bin near the door, he found a piece of cardboard that he ripped down to a piece that was small enough to keep the door from latching if he wedged it in place. Approaching the door again, he pushed on the opener as slowly and gently as he possibly could. He eased the door open and looked around the corner.

Nathan knew from coming here many times in the past that this door opened to a corridor that would take a 90^0 turn to his left and would lead to the offices in the old Hilo Hawaiian Hotel. Opposite that corridor was a small vestibule that had an opening that would empty onto what used to be a parking lot. He made his way down the corridor, looked to his left towards the offices, then turned in the other direction and stepped outside.

The quickest way to his house would be through the gardens. If he were to be seen here, no one would pay much attention to him even though he was just wearing shorts. People walked through the park in the evening all the time. It would be dark enough that his blond hair would not be too obvious, either.

It was an easy jog through the gardens to where Banyan Drive intersected Lihiwai Street. Now, he would have to pay more attention since there might be more people out and about. Lihiwai crossed Kamehameha Bikeway, which would be the busiest place he would have to navigate. There were many people on bicycles on Kam, but they were too busy with their own thoughts to notice a teenager out jogging, even in bare feet. Once he was on Manono Street, he felt safer since it was not so busy. It was only a few blocks up Manono, a left on Piilaui Street, and then just a couple of blocks more to his old home on Kalanikoa. A few minutes of light jogging brought him to the small house he grew up in. The small yard was dark, but he could see lights on in the kitchen and living room. He made his way to the steps of the back door and stood quietly for a moment. This was the part he feared. So, it was now or never; he knocked. And waited. He could hear someone coming; they were muttering, "Who it could be at this time of night?"

Nathan stood quite still as the door opened. It was Jonathan Ohana, his father. Jonathan looked at Nathan, took a step back, looked down, and shook his head. When he looked back up, there were tears in his eyes. He threw his arms around Nathan in a big bear hug and whispered in his ear, "It's you! It's really you!" He finally released his hold and stepped back, keeping his hands on Nathan's shoulders.

Lora called out, "Jonathan! Who is it?"

"Lora, we have a very special visitor!" Jonathan replied.

21
Not Enough Time

Jonathan brought Nathan into the living room. Laura looked up from her book and then stood up very slowly, as if in shock, because she was. Tears started to fill her eyes, and she shook her head slowly, not believing what she was seeing. Like Jonathan, she threw her arms around Nathan and kept saying in his ear, "I can't believe it! I can't believe it!"

"I don't want to let go of you," she said as she finally took a few steps back after releasing her hold on him. "I have so many questions. How did you get here? Where have you been?"

"I'm wondering the same thing," Jonathan said. "We really did believe you were not alive. We wanted to believe you were, but after so many years, I'm afraid we really did lose hope."

Nathan smiled and signed for them to sit down and that he would try to explain as much as possible. He also told them that he would have to keep things very short since he did not have much time.

Working backwards, he explained how he got into the dome through the submarine cavern and that he had help; that person was waiting just outside the entrance for him to return before the slack tide started to disappear.

"The reason I felt that I had to risk returning has to do with a threat to the dome," Nathan told them. "That threat is not from the people I have been living with, who are settled in a nice peaceful village not too far away, just to the north of here. The threat is there's an army coming from the other side of the island from a place called Cook. The man leading this army has fashioned himself to be the next Kamehameha, but his real name is Kawananakoa."

Nathan explained how his village came to know about Kawananakoa's plans to attack Hilo Dome and how they had been monitoring his activities. "He poses a threat not only to Hilo Dome, but to every village that exists on the island."

"There are more villages?" Jonathan asked.

"Kayli—she's the person waiting for me—and I discovered another small village just south of here. Given that, I'm sure there are many more all over the island. We have a lot of resources here on the windward side of the island that are apparently in very short supply on the leeward side."

Lora said, "It's funny for us to think about it that way. Inside the dome, we never think about where the wind is coming from or how it might affect how we live. But now I think we may have to face that reality. The environmental systems can't hold on much longer, especially with Hapuna and Teshima pressuring us to divert resources towards weapons."

"Kayli and I have watched the weapons training; it doesn't look very good. Kawananakoa's men are well-trained and well-armed. If the people in the dome are forced to fight on their own, I don't think the outcome will be good. That's why I needed to risk coming here now. Here's our plan."

Nathan described how they were now monitoring Kawananakoa, and that they had a good idea as to what his plans were. They just were not sure when they would be executed. "Dad, the two-pronged attack can be thwarted by you and your submarine team. Kawananakoa plans to send up to thirty *wa'a kaukahi* through the breakwater in Hilo Bay to attack the dome after the Hilo forces are engaged on the *mauka* side near the Wailuku River entrance."

"*Wa'a kaukahi?* You mean outriggers? Do you know how big they are?"

"They hold four men, so they're not too big," Nathan said. "They couldn't find *koa* trees big enough to construct larger canoes. Since they are relatively small, and we already know the subs can heavily damage *wa'a kaukahi* …"

Nathan paused here as Jonathan and Lora looked at each other. "Yes, I guess I need to ask you about that later. Anyway, the subs can be used as weapons to destroy as many canoes as possible."

Jonathan looked doubtful. "Yes, I'm sure they can damage the canoes and, yes, we have things to talk about regarding canoes, but how will I know where they are? I'm in the cavern and won't be able to see outside."

Nathan smiled. "I'll be there to help direct you. Kayli will be on the top of Coconut Island with a clear view out to the breakwater. She will be relaying information to me through thalk. That's what they call my special ability, to pick up thoughts and conversations. Everyone has it in the village of Honoli'i, and they all look sort of like me, too—sandy blond hair and green eyes. Do you think you can have all four subs operational soon?"

Jonathan nodded. "Yes, that shouldn't be a problem, and I know we have the personnel who can run them all at once. How will we know when to deploy them?"

Nathan said, "As I said to begin with, I don't have much time. I'll have to leave soon, but I'll come back when we detect the army is on its way. As soon as we see them start to come towards the dome, I'll come back, and we can start coordinating when to use the subs when Kayli arrives."

Lora had not said a word during this exchange, but now she had a question for Nathan. "Do you know what they are going to do on the *mauka* side of the dome to initiate the attack? I doubt that they could penetrate through the panels with the weapons they have."

"From what we figure, they are going to cause enough damage where the river comes in to shut down the environmental systems, so there would be no electricity, no air circulation, and no pumps to supply water to the people. In other words, they plan a siege that would cause Hapuna and Teshima to open the panels to the outside. Once that happens, the inside of the dome will be vulnerable, and Teshima will have to deploy his men to stop them." Nathan stopped there and thought for a minute. "Just how many men does Teshima have? It better be more than the police force he had when I left."

Lora said, "It's not much more. Hapuna and Teshima tried to initiate a draft, but it was met with a lot of resistance. Their plan was to aggressively attack the people you have been living with. They thought that someone from Honoli'i shot one of their men when they were outside the dome, and they have used that as a way to stir up some hatred against the people we have been calling the Ferals."

"That shot was actually taken by one of the spies Kawananakoa sent. Our people were there when it happened and captured one spy and killed the other. That's how we got started tracking Kawananakoa and figuring out their plans. We brought the prisoner to the village, and his thoughts just gave him away. He still doesn't know that we got so much information from him."

"How many men does Kawananakoa have?" Jonanthan asked.

"Our best estimate is around three hundred. Over one hundred will be in the canoe attack after the larger force engages the dome from the *mauka* side."

Jonathan was shaking his head. "There's no way we have the people and weaponry to defend the dome against something like that."

"That's where my friends from Honoli'i come in again. Not only will we be giving you help directing the subs, our village will be sending a small army to come in from behind Kawananakoa's men in a surprise attack. Our people are very stealthy and excellent shots with crossbows and bows and arrows. I really believe the dome will not fall to Kawananakoa."

Nathan looked at his parents, realizing that he was about to leave them once again. "I can't tell you how much I worried about you and how badly I felt knowing that you thought I was dead." Now, tears were in his eyes. "But I have to leave now. Kayli is waiting."

Nathan stood up to leave and held his arms open to embrace his parents. As the three of them hugged each other, Jonathan said, "I'm coming with you."

Nathan backed away from the group hug and signed, "There's no way you can do that. You have to get the subs ready."

Jonathan smiled. "No, I didn't mean I was going to go back to the village with you. I'll bike along with you to the submarine docks to make sure you get away safely."

"I'd really like that," said Nathan. He hugged his mother again. "I'll be back in about two weeks. We think that Kawananakoa will try to mount his attack at the next full moon. The tides should be low enough for me to get back a day or two before that. Then, we will have lots of things to talk about, and I have a lot of people I want you to meet."

Lora said, "I'm guessing one of them is Kayli."

"Yes, Mom. One of them is Kayli." He added, "I love you and miss you."

Before Nathan could leave, there was a knock on the front door.

"Lora! Jonathan! I need to talk with you. It's important." It was Chief Teshima.

"Dad, you stay here with Mom and let Teshima in. As soon as he is in the living room, I'll slip out the back and get to the submarines."

Nathan quietly moved into the kitchen and opened the door slightly, ready to move. Jonathan opened the door to find Teshima there with one of his men.

"Come in, Chief. It must be important for you to be here at this time of night."

Teshima said, "We had a report that someone was seen running down your street earlier. A young man with no shirt or shoes. You wouldn't know anything about this person, would you?"

With that, Nathan slipped out the back door only to find one of Teshima's men in the back yard peering into the small shed. Nathan had not been spotted yet, so he gently grabbed the handlebars of a bike that was leaning against the house by the door and eased it towards the street on the opposite side of the yard. Just as he swung his leg over the bike to mount it, he heard Teshima's man yell, "Stop! You there on the bike! Halt!"

Nathan had no plans to halt. He was on the bike and racing down the street, retracing his steps to the submarine base. He could only hope that Teshima would not guess where he was going. A place run by his father was probably one of the last places they would look if they suspected that it was, in fact, Jonathan's son that had been spotted coming back to his home.

Chief Teshima tried to move into the kitchen from the living room, but Jonathan stepped in front of him. He put his hand on the Chief's chest and said, "You're right, Chief Teshima. We DO have some important things to talk about."

Nathan easily outdistanced the officer he left in his backyard. He crossed over Kamememeha and zoomed through Lili'uokalani Park to the sub base entrance. He stuck the bike in the rack outside the door and sprinted down the corridor, hoping that his piece of cardboard was still in place keeping the lock open.

It was.

Ignoring the ladder, Nathan ran down the walkway to the bow of the sub and, with just a quick look back at the door, jumped in the water. There was just enough light to spot the entrance to the cave and his way to safety. He flipped on his back and started frog-kicking his way out, the whole time thinking, "Kayli! On my way out! Kayli! On my way out!"

22
Facing Reality

There was no light at the end of the tunnel. The darkness of the bay under a new moon was complete, but Nathan became aware of his impending exit from the cave without needing his vision. He could hear the lapping of the light waves against the mouth of the cave as he approached the outside; he was ready for this chapter of his life to be over.

During his swim out, he reflected on his last two experiences in Hilo Dome. Both involved being chased by Teshima and his men, and the end result of both chases was the same; Nathan was out in Hilo Bay. However, this time someone was waiting for him.

As he came out of the mouth of the cave, Nathan flipped on his stomach and took a quick look around.

"Straight ahead, Nathan!"

He could now make out the silhouette of Kayli sitting in their *wa'a kaukahi* just ten meters in front of him. He swam over to her and popped his head up on the port side between the outrigger and the hull. He gripped the rim of the hull and pulled himself over the side, tumbling rather ungracefully into the boat.

"Nice entrance," Kayli said.

"Hey, I'm not looking for style points. I just want to get back to our shelter and get some sleep."

Kayli reached out and touched his shoulder. "I'm so glad you're back safely. Never having been in the dome, I had no idea what you were facing in there."

"It went pretty smoothly, except for my exit," Nathan laughed. "It was oddly reminiscent of my last departure. *Déjà vu* all over again."

"Huh?"

"Oh, I'll explain when we get back. It was something I read in one of my books that was about famous quotes."

"You did a lot of reading when you lived in the dome, didn't you? I guess you miss it a lot."

"Well, yeah, I did a lot of reading, and I do miss it, but there's so much to do in the village, and I've learned so much from you and your family. I do like my life in Honoli'i. A lot! I feel like I finally really fit in somewhere. And, while I miss my parents and it was tough seeing and leaving them again, I know it won't be too long until we will be able to move freely from our village to Hilo Dome and back again." Nathan paused. "At least that's what I think will happen."

They got back to their cove, stowed the *wa'a kaukahi*, and turned in to get an early start on the following day. They needed to let the village know that they were successful in reaching Nathan's parents.

***

Jonathan and Lora sat with Chief Teshima in their living room. Teshima could see from Jonathan's face and his actions that he had better pay attention to him, especially after Jonathan had forcibly pushed him into an armchair in the living room. At that point, Teshima sent his two men home. It was obvious they would not catch Nathan, at least not right away. He had a lot of questions for the two of them, but he thought it would be best if Jonathan or Lora spoke first.

After a long silence, Jonathan said, "I guess you know who our visitor was."

Teshima nodded. "When we received a report from someone who was biking on Kamehameha that they had seen a teenager with blond hair crossing the road, we figured it had to be Nathan. Is that the first time you have seen him since, you know, since we forced him to jump into the river?"

"Yes, it was a total surprise. We're glad it took so long for the report to get to you and for you to act on it since Nathan had a lot of important things to tell us relating to Hilo Dome and the dangers we all face," Lora said.

"I'm guessing you won't tell me how he got here."

Jonathan said, "I think for now, that will just stay in the family."

Lora picked up where she had left off. "As I was saying, we are all in a lot of danger. Not from the Ferals, as you call them, who live just outside the dome, but from an individual with an army who is intent on getting our resources and probably conscripting men for his army to try to conquer the rest of the island.

According to Nathan, there are probably quite a few villages out there, and they are probably not prepared to defend themselves against an organized army."

Teshima looked from Lora to Jonathan and then back to Lora. "So, you mean I was right about aggressive people living outside the dome?"

Jonathan shook his head. "You were right, but in the wrong way. If you had had your way, you would have attacked a very peaceful village, a village that has been living successfully in harmony with their surroundings. In doing so, you would have committed a terrible wrong against totally innocent people, people who want to be our allies in defeating Kawananakoa, the man leading the army. You and Mayor Hapuna were so concerned about remaining in power and keeping control of Hilo Dome that you nearly cost us everything."

Lora said, "This Kawananakoa, or Kamehameha VI as he calls himself, really set you up by shooting one of your men on one of your outside the dome excursions. He played that card very well."

Teshima nodded. "Yes, I guess he did." He sat, looking down at his feet. "So, what do we do now?"

Lora and Jonathan proceeded to tell him the plans developed by Sam Pahinui and the people of Honoliʻi as described by Nathan. As they went through the plans, Teshima nodded every so often, finally looking up at the two of them, thoroughly engaged in what they had to say.

"So, it sounds as though we have to commit to using most of our force to engage them in a fight when they attack by the river on the *mauka* side, and we have to count on you and your men, Jonathan, to take care of the attacking outriggers in the bay." Teshima added, "I guess it's up to me to convince the mayor that this is what we need to do."

Lora said, "How tough do you think that will be?"

"Well, if it means whether Hilo Dome will survive as a city or be taken over by some outsiders, I don't think he has a choice. I'm just not sure our men are up to it."

"Well," Jonathan said, "don't forget that shortly after the fighting starts, Kawananakoa is going to find himself in a really tough spot. I imagine the people who will be sent from Honoliʻi are well-trained with their weapons. After all, it's how they survive, how they get their food. Plus, they have some unique ways of communicating."

Jonathan proceeded to explain how Nathan could thalk and that all the members of the village of Honoli'i could do the same thing. Teshima's mouth started to open more and more as he understood what this meant.

"So, this is how it all started when Nathan overheard—well, he didn't overhear, Nathan intercepted what the mayor and I were discussing when you brought him to work. Is that right, Lora?"

"I think that's the most likely explanation," Lora said.

Teshima was shaking his head again. "All those years ago, all the pain and anguish we caused you and how we put Nathan in danger. I don't know how you can ever forgive me and the mayor. Yes, we were being greedy, but I thought we were doing the right thing. I guess we were not. I can't speak for Hapuna, but I am asking for your forgiveness now. I am truly sorry for all the trouble I have caused you. I just don't know how I can make it up to you."

Jonathan smiled slightly. "Well, you can start by convincing Mayor Hapuna that we need to follow this plan that we just described and that if we win—excuse me, *when* we win the battle—Hilo Dome will be returned to a democracy, and we will have peaceful relations with our neighbors."

Chief Teshima stood and extended his hand to Jonathan. As they shook hands, Teshima said, "I'll make sure that this is what happens." He then extended his hand to Lora. As they shook, he said, "Again, I am so sorry for all that has happened."

Lora said, "As things have turned out, it's for the better. We would have never known about the pending attack if Nathan had not been in Honoli'i. Let's just make sure that all his work and the work of the people from the village is not in vain."

Teshima said, "I'll make sure."

***

Alfred Kawananakoa was not pleased with the progress being made on the construction of the *wa'a kaukahi*. After the completion of the first ten, progress slowed due to the lack of *koa* logs large enough to form the hull. His men had to move farther and farther up the mountainside to get the logs, and then they had to partially hollow them out to haul them all the way down to the beach at Hā'ena. He had wanted at least twenty completed by this time, but that was not to be.

However, they still had time. Ten were in the water and being used for training, and another ten were nearly ready to be fitted with outriggers. *I'll get my thirty, but it will take a lot more work,* he thought.

Kawananakoa also sent a contingent of men to cut down two or three of the biggest trees they could find close to the waterfall, just above the point where the Wailuku entered the dome. They did not need to be *koa* trees; any tree with a straight trunk would do. More than likely, the trees would be Australian pines. The trees grew very tall, up to thirty meters, and were extremely common. He was not too concerned about this aspect of the attack plan. There was plenty of time to get the logs trimmed and ready for their run down the Wailuku.

Kawananakoa called for Holokai Bishop, his designated "admiral," to meet him at the beach where the canoes were being assembled. "Holokai, I think we will break away two of our training canoes for a run down to Hilo Bay. We need to get some reliable times to coordinate the arrival of our *wa'a kaukahi* with our attack on the dome itself."

"Two canoes should give us a good estimate," Bishop said. "But remember, thirty canoes will move considerably slower. If it takes more than a day, we'll need to scout out some places where we might pull ashore and spend the night if we are to attack sometime the following day."

"Yes, I think that might be a necessity," Kawananakoa agreed. "We want our men to be well-rested before they arrive at the breakwater."

"I'll go find eight men and tell them to be ready to set off at first light. Hopefully, the seas will be relatively calm tomorrow. We certainly don't want to lose any men or *wa'a kaukahi* before the assault."

Kawananakoa nodded. "Absolutely. I'm counting on you to get this done."

The two watchers from Honoli'i overheard this exchange and headed back to their factory shelter. It certainly seemed to them that Kawananakoa and his men were trying to be ready to attack at the next full moon. Their relief watchers were due to arrive tomorrow, and they would be able to get this information back to Sam quickly. The time for action was getting close.

23
The Wait

Kayli and Nathan returned to Honoli'i and told Sam all about Nathan's visit with his parents.

"It sounds like you had a successful reunion with them," Sam said. "I can't imagine how they must have felt after all this time."

"It was pretty emotional," Nathan said. "Unfortunately, we didn't have a lot of time to talk about things like that although I really wanted to describe how wonderful my life has been since I arrived in Honoli'i. I told them they would have plenty of time to get to know you and the Pahinui family and all the people here in the village after we settle things with Kawananakoa. I'm not sure how things are going to work out between them and Chief Teshima. I couldn't really stick around to see how that turned out."

Sam nodded. "Yeah, you didn't have much of a choice there, but I bet if your parents get the chance to explain how this all came about and what needs to be done, Teshima will have to come around. I'm assuming he's not an idiot."

Kayli asked, "When are the next watchers due back in the village? I'd really like to know how much time we have before we have to set things in motion."

"You and me both," Sam said. "I'm expecting them to return sometime this afternoon. I'm hoping we have a better picture as to how far along Kawananakoa is with his canoe construction and training." He looked in the direction of the path leading out of the village towards Hilo Dome as if he could draw them in. "Anyway, let's grab a bite to eat while we wait, and then I need to double-check our own forces. Edward Park has been organizing the men. They've also been constructing a lot of new crossbows. We definitely want to have the upper hand in all aspects of this battle."

They headed for the Pahinui *hale* to get something to eat and await the return of the watchers. When they arrived at the *hale*, they were greeted by Layla Pahinui.

She smiled and said, "You're in luck if you're looking for lunch. Byl and Aaron had some good luck trapping *ula*. They caught enough spiny lobster for everyone in the family."

Nathan's mouth began to water at the mere mention of *ula*. It was a prized catch, and the people of the village would only trap them at certain times of the year. Female spiny lobster with eggs were always tossed back. Nathan really loved the way Auntie Bernice prepared her *ula* and served it with *limu inamona* salad. The people living in the dome never got to experience eating seaweed since no one ever went out to collect it. And they certainly never had lobster! Nathan really wanted to have his parents experience all the new foods he had come to love while living with the Pahinuis.

After finishing lunch, Sam Pahinui went to find Edward Park. He located Edward behind his butcher shop putting the finishing touches on a new crossbow.

"That's beauty," Sam said admiringly. "The grain on that is exquisite."

Edward beamed. "Thanks. It's made from an *'ōhi'a lehua* tree. In fact, most of the new crossbows we've been making use wood from the same tree."

"If there's enough of it left, I'd like to make one for Kayli and another for Nathan. It'll be a nice reward for all the hard work they've been putting in."

"There's plenty left," Edward said. "Yeah, I heard Kayli and Nathan made it back. Is it true Nathan went into Hilo Dome and reunited with his parents?"

Sam looked surprised. "Wow! Word really does get around quickly here in the village. He had a little difficulty during his departure, but nothing serious. He shared all the important information with his parents before Teshima interrupted things." He paused and looked around. "Jeffrey's one of the watchers coming back today, right? Any sign of him?"

Edward looked up from his bow and pointed to the path out of the village. "As a matter of fact, here he comes now with Sonny Choy. Sonny will be going back out with someone new since Jeffrey's finishing his second shift."

"Aloha, Jeffrey and Sonny! Welcome back," Sam said. "I hope your trip wasn't too difficult."

Jeffrey smiled. "Nah, it was easy. Byl and Aaron really found a good place for us watchers to stay, and our observation area for the beach seemed really safe. Speaking of the beach, it appears that Kawananakoa will be ready to make his attack in two weeks. Their final approach to the location above the dome will be on a full moon. From what we saw, they will have thirty canoes ready to launch."

"That's pretty much what we were expecting," Sam said. "I think we'll be ready to play our part. I'm just hoping that the people in Hilo Dome are ready to do theirs. *Mahalo* to both of you for volunteering to do this. The information you are gathering is crucial to getting the timing just right."

"Glad to help!" Jeffrey turned to Sonny and said, "Okay, let's get some lunch. I'm starved."

As the boys walked away, Edward looked sad. "I just hope everyone we love makes it through all this."

Sam nodded. "I agree. We're taking a lot of risks here, but I don't think there's any way this village could survive if we don't step in to help. As I said, the people of Hilo Dome need to be ready to shoulder some of the burden as well."

***

Jonathan gathered all his people in one of the conference rooms in the old Hilo Hawaiian Hotel. There were two rooms that had been conference rooms, and there was a huge dining room just above them that was no longer used for serving food. Jonathan liked to use this room for his meetings since it had a sweeping view of Hilo Bay where all the pens were located and where the invaders from Cook would be trying to get into the bay and then inside the dome.

"We are going to need all hands on deck for this one," Jonathan said as he looked around the room at people he had worked with all his life. "We will be under attack by probably thirty *waʻa kaukahi*, each containing four men. It will be our task to prevent them from landing outside the dome. In fact, I don't want ANY of the canoes to make it past our position here at Coconut Island."

Harry Kwon, Jonathan's chief engineer, raised his hand. "Sub 3 is stripped down in the middle of an engine overhaul. It will take at least a week to get it back together and operational. Do we have that much time?"

Jonathan nodded. "We believe they will attack in about two weeks during the next full moon. That should give you enough time to get things back together. I'm assuming the other three are in good shape."

"Yes, sir. We were planning on a pen harvest tomorrow so Subs 1 and 2 are ready to go and 4 will be our stand-by. Not expecting any problems."

"Good!" Jonathan turned to his chief electrician. "We need to ensure all the tracking devices and viewing screens are in sync. After the harvest, we can do a few test runs. When we're doing the test runs, our pilots will be working on coordinating the movement of the subs. When Sub 3 is ready, we'll have to do some training. We've never had four boats operating at the same time. The last thing we want to have happen is a collision between our own craft."

Kerry Parker, his lead pilot had a question. "We can get the boats ready, and we can practice our maneuvers, but how are we going to know where the *wa'a kaukahi* are? They move; our pens don't."

"Good question, Kerry." Jonathan paused for a bit before continuing. "I have some very special news for you all. We found out about this attack from someone you knew from years ago—my son, Nathan."

Harry asked, "Nathan's alive? Nathan was in the dome?"

"That's right, Harry. My son is alive. He has been living in a village not too far from the dome. The people of the village intercepted and captured some spies from the invading army from Cook and learned of their plans. They have been keeping track of them ever since. Once they knew how the army was planning its attack, Nathan swam through the cave and made it to our house to tell Lora and me, and then I told Chief Teshima."

"I'm still confused," Harry said. "How does that help us in knowing where the canoes are?"

Jonathan sighed. This might be hard for them to swallow. "My son and all the people in the village of Honoli'i, the village where he has been living, have what amounts to something similar to telepathy."

As Jonathan expected, murmurs swept through the conference room. He waited for them to die down.

"If you recall, my son cannot talk, but he does have the ability to intercept thoughts and relatively distant conversations. This is how the villagers communicate with each other. They call it 'Thalk' or think/talk. Nathan will be in the control room with us, and one of his friends will be on top of the dome of Coconut Island acting as a spotter. They will be relaying information to us so that we will be able to guide the subs in a way that will do the most damage. Nathan will be pointing to our screens indicating where their fleet is in real time."

Kerry said, "I'm guessing you have a plan of attack, right, Boss?"

Jonathan smiled. "Right you are, Kerry. As all of you know, there is a breakwater extending about two-thirds of the way across the entrance to Hilo Bay. It's what keeps our pens relatively safe from any serious wave action most of the time. Their canoes will be at their most vulnerable right when they have to enter through the opening in the breakwater. I would like to have our subs side by side and heading out to sea from the bay. They will be running underwater at this time. When we get the word from our spotter that the *wa'a kaukahi* are right at the breakwater, I want our subs to surface under the lead boats and then head out to sea into the rest of them. We will continue to make passes back and forth through the breakwater until we get the word that most of the canoes have been shattered or capsized. Our spotter will then help us pick off any stragglers that any have slipped through. Any questions?"

Jonathan gave them a minute or two, but no questions came forward. "I'm sure you'll have some as the day progresses. I'll be spending my time in the sub cavern, if you need me. *Mahalo* to all of you. As you can imagine, getting this right is of the utmost importance."

***

While Jonathan was working hard on getting all the submarines up and running, Chief Teshima had the difficult task of convincing Mayor Hapuna that the threat was real, but it was not what he expected it to be.

Mayor Hapuna paced angrily back and forth in his office in front of Teshima. It was difficult for Teshima to watch since even this little bit of "exercise" was causing Hapuna to wheeze and gasp for breath.

"So, you're telling me that we won't be launching an attack on the Ferals," Hapuna said without looking directly at Teshima. "Instead, a totally different group of Ferals will be launching an attack on us at some unknown time in the near future. On top of that, we'll be dependent on and indebted to the Ferals we were planning to exterminate. Do I have that correct?"

Chief Teshima said, "That's correct, Mayor Hapuna. Our best course of action now is to figure out how we can best defend the dome. Our weapons training has not achieved all we wanted it to, and we are lagging in our weapons production. I'm afraid the only thing we have to our advantage right now is that it looks as though the fighting will be in close rather than at a distance, so our electric pistols will be effective. It might even create a panic in Kawananakoa's men when we discharge them. I'm sure they haven't seen anything like them before."

Hapuna fumed even more. "I don't like it. We've lost control. We've lost the upper hand. Even if we win this battle, Hilo Dome will never be the same."

"I think you have that right," Teshima agreed. "But there's not a whole lot we can do about it."

Teshima let that hang there for a moment as he tried to figure out how he was going to break the news to Mayor Hapuna that when—if—they won the battle, the citizens were going to demand new elections with a more democratic approach to the government than had been in place over the past twenty or so years. Martial law would no longer be tolerated. New departments within the government would have to be established to deal with external relations, the development of resources outside the physical limits of the dome, and possibly lifting the limits on family size.

"Mayor Hapuna, if you could stop pacing for a moment, there is an even more serious issue that I need to discuss with you."

Hapuna stopped and looked at Teshima. "What do you mean 'more serious?' What could be more serious than an attack on Hilo Dome?"

"Well," Teshima started slowly, "the people of Hilo Dome, if our defense of the dome is successful, are going to demand open elections, the elimination of our martial law."

Mayor Hapuna slammed his fist down on his desk. "What are you talking about? We'll still have the police force; we'll still control the weapons."

"That's not exactly true, Mayor." Now Teshima began pacing. "We are arming A LOT of our citizens to defend the dome. There's no practical way to get those weapons back without threatening physical force. Do you plan to instigate a civil war after we just fought against what they will all view as a common enemy? They have also threatened to strike. There will be slow-downs in farming, slow-downs in *kāhala* harvest, and reductions in generation of electrical power, if we have any. In other words, we will be 'in control' in name only."

Hapuna slumped down into his chair behind his desk. "So, you're saying it's over for us."

"As things exist now? Yes." Teshima stopped pacing and looked squarely at Hapuna. "But I still have a job to do. We still have to defend the dome."

Chief Teshima began to explain to a defeated-looking Mayor Hapuna what all the defense plans were, from the use of the submarines to defend the bay to the coordinated attack on Kawananakoa's force from the rear by the people of Honoli'i. Hapuna showed little interest. He did not even look at Teshima; he simply stared at the wall directly opposite his desk. He was lost in his own world of self-pity. It became obvious to Teshima as he went on that Mayor Hapuna was a defeated man and would be of no use in making sure all the defense plans were initiated. Probably for the best, he thought. He finished what he had to say, gave Hapuna time to respond and, hearing nothing, left Hapuna's office, possibly for the last time.

PART 3
The Siege

24
Setting the Trap

Byl and Aaron had cycled back to being watchers at Kawananakoa's camp. It was just a few days before the full moon, and they wanted to be on site to see if the army was going to start to mobilize. They were not disappointed in their assumption.

Kawananakoa was directing his army to start breaking down the camp in preparation for the short march to Keaau and then the final push to Hilo Dome. They had no plans to return to Hā'ena or to Keaau after the battle. With no thoughts of defeat, Kawananakoa expected his land force would unite with his sea force inside Hilo Dome and secure it as theirs. Of course, he was totally unaware that the people of Hilo Dome had been alerted to the impending attack and were in the final preparations of creating a defense.

Holokai Bishop was conducting some final training with his men in their *wa'a kaukahi*. For the past few days, all thirty canoes had been in the ocean conducting coordinated maneuvers. Bishop had already decided to be in the lead boat, but he had yet to determine the exact order and formation of the others. It would all come down to what worked out the best in the trials they were conducting. He was surprised that all thirty of the *wa'a kaukahi* had been completed, the last one just a day before he wanted to start his full flotilla training. Kawananakoa had been pleased, and this, in turn, pleased Bishop.

At the same time, Akuma Kuwabara had been conditioning his men and conducting his own exercises in the wooded areas to the south of Hā'ena. He had been using an old derelict warehouse to simulate Hilo Dome. It was far smaller than the actual target, but his men would get the general idea as to how to deploy themselves and conduct an attack.

Unfortunately, this was what Byl and Aaron were hoping to see, but since they were north of Hā'ena, there was no way to safely circumnavigate the Kawananakoa encampment to get to the south side. The force from Honoli'i would have to continue to plan their counterattack based on the assumption that Kawananakoa would approach from the *mauka* side where the Wailuku entered the dome.

In the late afternoon after, the various military exercises had been completed and the men settled into breaking down the camp in earnest, Kawananakoa met with Kuwabara and Bishop on the beach where all the canoes were located. Byl and Aaron were close enough to pick up the conversation.

"We will move out tomorrow," Kawananakoa said. "Kuwabara and I will lead our men up to Keaau and make camp there for the night. The next day, we will move into position around the dome. Before dawn, we will launch the ramming logs down the river. If all goes as planned, this will shut down the electric grid inside the dome and send the people into a panic. Then, we wait. I expect that by midday, it will become extremely hot and stuffy inside the dome. With no power, the temperatures will soar. They should have to open the panels just to make it livable.

When they do, we will light a fire to create a smoke signal that will tell you, Bishop, that the land attack is on as scheduled."

Bishop nodded in agreement. "We have a place picked out close to the entrance of the bay where we plan to camp for the night. It should only take us an hour or so to get to the entrance at the breakwater."

"In that case, you should probably get underway as soon as you see our signal," Kawananakoa said. "That should give us enough time to become fully engaged with the people in the dome on our side. I expect that you should be able to move right into the town with minimal resistance. Your job will then be to occupy and secure as much of the main part of the city as possible on your way to attacking the people fighting with us. That should give them a rude surprise!"

He turned to look at Kuwabara. "Akuma, once we get encamped at Keaau, I want you to continue on towards Hilo Dome. Our scouts located a set of buildings that some of our men have been using as a base to prepare the ramming logs. It's right near the falls. I want you to make sure all those preparations have been completed. It is a secure and well-defended base, so I'm not expecting any trouble there. They have had plenty of time to get two or three trees felled and trimmed. They should be ready."

Byl and Aaron had heard enough. Both were concerned that they had overlooked this secondary base near the falls. They decided to leave immediately to get word back to Honoli'i. They knew that Nathan had to have enough time to get back inside the dome to tell his father to make the final preparations for launching the submarines. They would not be able to get all the way back to their village before nightfall, but they should be able to get far enough so that they would arrive late in the morning the next day.

**

While Kawananakoa was in his final planning stage for the attack, Sam Pahinui and Edward Park were leading a group of twenty men and women, all the best archers in the village, to a position several kilometers upstream from the big waterfall. Sam knew of a second set of falls there with an area where they could ford the river. They were there to scout out the best areas of concealment, near enough so that they could close on Kawananakoa quickly, but far enough upstream to keep them from being discovered.

They located a place to ford upstream from the falls. The water was moving swiftly there, but there were plenty of boulders and shallows for them to cross safely. This looked to be the best entry point for them to come in behind Kawananakoa's force.

Sam gathered everyone together after they were all across. "Each of you will have three people assigned to you. Right now, we are going to move down closer to the dome. You have to remain alert since we believe there are some of Kawananakoa's men here. Edward and I will work with you to find positions where each of you will be located. Then, I would like you to find positions for the three people who will be with you. You are looking for places of concealment that will let you fire your weapons at the enemy but without being fully exposed. You've all done this enough when you are out hunting. The problem this time is that your prey can fire back at you. Our first assault has to be the most effective. They will be engaged in battle, looking in towards the dome. Make your first shot count."

"Just as in hunting *pua'a*," Edward chimed in, "if you miss your first shot, your prey will be startled. Unlike in hunting *pua'a*, this prey will not run away."

"Hold your fire until I send the command," Sam continued. "We will be sending eighty arrows and crossbow bolts simultaneously. If we are accurate, and if our estimates are correct, we would be able to take out at least forty to fifty of their men. That's pretty optimistic, but it will be our goal. Obviously, the more we take out at first, the safer we are and the safer the people of Hilo Dome will be. Any questions? Let's move down."

Moving twenty-two people as quietly as possible through some dense vegetation was a difficult task, but all the men and women were experienced hunters, accomplished in being stealthy enough to not startle skittish prey. They continued down the gentle slope. Sam halted them when they were about one hundred meters from the falls. They could see people moving around several large buildings between them and the falls. Their final destination, Hilo Dome, was just beyond.

Sam said, "It looks like we're not going to be able to get any closer. I really wanted us to find the actual positions for when we begin our attack, but that's not going to happen."

"The vegetative cover doesn't change much moving downslope to the dome," Edward said. We can simulate being in position here. At least we can practice how we are going to arrange our formation to be most effective when we actually do fire our first volley."

Sam split the group in half with ten going with him and ten joining Edward farther out to the right. Each group moved quietly as they formed a firing line that would have each archer about two to three meters from the next archer. The irregularities of the cover made it impossible to be precise, but good cover was more important than precision in spacing. After about an hour, Sam had everyone meet back at the ford.

"Our plan is to be in position the night before the planned attack. We will arrive here in late afternoon just before sunset. Be prepared to settle in overnight. I know this is nothing new for you people; you've all had to do this at one time or another when you have been out hunting. However, some of the people with you may not have had the pleasure of camping out under the stars. Make sure you talk with them about what it is like and what they need to bring." Sam paused and looked at each of the people with him. "I'm leaving it up to each individual to decide what provisions they need to bring with them. Most importantly, make sure your weapons are in good shape and that every person has a knife. I don't expect you to need a knife, but it's always best to have one in case things get ugly. Okay, let's head back to the village."

They forded the river and made good time getting back to Honoli'i. When they arrived, Byl and Aaron were waiting for them with information that confirmed the attack was going to proceed as they had anticipated.

25
Déjà Vu All Over Again

Byl and Aaron met with Sam, Edward, Nathan, and Kayli at the Pahinui *hale*.

After they described what they had seen just before leaving, Sam said, "Okay, Nathan, it's time to get you back inside."

Nathan said, "Kayli and I need to get over to the cave entrance to try to figure out when low tide is. That's the only time I can get in."

Kayli added, "This time, I'm coming in with you too."

"I'm not sure that's a good idea," Sam said. "We don't know how things stand inside the dome. What if Nathan's parents were arrested by Teshima and taken into custody? You could be walking into a very dangerous situation."

"We can swim in as far as the opening of the cave into the main area of the submarine base," Nathan suggested. "At that point, we should be able to watch for a few minutes to see if everything looks normal, and by 'normal,' I mean if it looks like they are getting the subs and the base ready to defend the bay. If something doesn't look right, we can simply swim back out. No one would want to follow us to the outside."

"I still don't like it," Sam said, shaking his head.

"If they aren't getting prepared, we have to get that information back to you as soon as possible," Kayli said, "because, if they aren't getting prepared, that means they won't be defending the *mauka* side of the dome, and if they're not doing that, they won't be engaged with Kawananakoa's men when you and our people are going to attack. The element of surprise will be blown."

Sam had no response for that. He looked at his daughter, then at Nathan, and finally over to Edward, who was sitting just to his left. "Well, Edward, what do you think?"

"I think Kayli has made a very valid point. This all falls apart if the people of Hilo Dome are not responding to the information Nathan gave to his parents." He looked over at Nathan. "You're the only one who has been there. I think we have to trust your judgement. It does give us an opportunity to make sure the dome is getting ready."

"There's another reason I need to go in," Kayli added. "I would have to spend the night sitting on top of the Coconut Island dome, or at least nearby. I'm not sure I want to do that alone."

Sam sighed. "Okay. Okay. You'll both be going in. But if anything looks out of place at all in terms of what they are doing in that sub base, you need to leave immediately."

Aaron asked, "What if the next low tide isn't until tonight? Will they be working on the subs then?"

"I would think they will be working around the clock if my parents were successful in convincing everyone," Nathan said. "It would be best to get in during the day to make the most accurate assessment. That's just one thing we'll have to play by ear."

Byl laughed. "Well, at least we know from your guitar playing that you DO know how to play by ear."

"That's funny," Nathan said. "I thought I used my fingers."

Everyone laughed, and Sam said, "On that note (ha, ha) the two of you need to leave as soon as possible. If you can get in this afternoon, that would be best."

Their small meeting broke up, and Kayli and Nathan went to gather their things. They would not need much. Either they were going to get inside and stay inside until Kayli needed to take her spotting post, or they would be turning around and coming back to Honoli'i immediately.

***

Kayli and Nathan headed down to the beach and pulled their *wa'a kaukahi* out from where it was stored. They put what little equipment they had in the canoe and shoved off from the beach. Conditions were not ideal. There was some heavy surf they had to plow through and small white caps out in the open water. It was nothing they could not handle, but it might slow them up a bit. It seemed close to low tide, but it was hard to tell if it was coming in or going out with all the wave action hitting the beach.

It was late afternoon by the time they arrived at the mouth of the cave leading into the submarine base. The gap between the water and the top of the cave was not as great as when Nathan swam it the first time, but it looked like they could make a safe passage. They pulled the canoe ashore at the small beach Kayli had discovered the last time Nathan went in.

They both strapped knives to their legs and then clambered up the hill leading to the crest of the Coconut Island dome. Nathan could see that this would indeed give Kayli a great view of the breakwater entrance, and it had plenty of cover. Behind some vegetation, Kayli left a couple of mats and a thin covering she could use when she came back the night before they expected the attack to occur.

They walked down a gentle slope to the area where the cave entrance should be. When they could go no farther, they dropped to all fours and crept carefully to the edge. There was no telling how stable the land was here.

Peering over the edge, they could see that it was about a three-meter drop to the water and that the edge of the island sloped slightly outward. The area they were standing on seemed to be solid lava rock, so they stood so they could jump far enough out to land in deep water. Nathan grabbed Kayli's hand.

"On three?" Kayli nodded. "One! Two! Three!"

They landed rather ungracefully in the water, but at least it was a safe splash down. They popped up and swam to the entrance. Nathan described how he swam on his back last time using a frog kick and that he kept one hand on the ceiling as much as possible.

"I'll go first," he said. "I know what it will be like when we emerge on the other side."

"Sounds good to me. Lead the way!"

Nathan flipped over and entered the cave with Kayli following close behind.

***

Lora was standing with some of her engineers looking out at the three turbines that generated power for Hilo Dome. Knowing that they were vulnerable to the planned attack from Kawananakoa, they had been working non-stop since Nathan's visit to try to find a way to protect the blades that spun in the water. They had no way to manufacture new metal protective struts. That would have been the best solution. They talked about large wooden barriers outside the dome, but there was no way to anchor them in the river, and even if they could find a way to do that, the barrier would interfere with the flow of water, the power necessary for the generators to be effective.

Even though the blades on all three turbines were turning, one generator was always "offline" for maintenance. Not that the maintenance was doing much good anymore. There were no more replacement parts. They had come to the point where they would have to cannibalize one of the generators just to keep two up and running. Lora and her team had run out of options.

"I'm afraid we're just going to have to let the attack happen," Lora said to her team. "We were reaching the point where we were going to have to open the dome anyway. Mayor Hapuna and Chief Teshima had been planning this for some time. At least with their plan, we would be giving up on the turbines on our own terms."

One of the engineers asked, "Where is Hapuna, anyway? As far as I know, no one has seen him for days."

"He's holed up in his office all the time," Laura said. "He's not doing anything to run the dome on a day-to-day basis, and as far as I know, he has no visitors. Chief Teshima has pretty much assumed all the duties of both mayor and as the head of our defenses. He's done a decent job, but he's starting to show the strain of managing everything by himself. Most of the divisions are operating simply under the direction of each division chair. For example, I've barely seen Jonathan over the past week. He's been at the sub base getting the boats ready to defend the bay."

While Lora and her engineers were frustrated on one side of the dome, Jonathan and his team were making great progress in the sub base at the other side. They had been putting in long hours getting the submarines ready. All four were up and running, and they had had the opportunity to test them all earlier in the week. They had even tried some of the tactical maneuvers Jonathan had planned. The subs, the tracking devices, and the controls had all operated flawlessly.

***

Nathan sensed that he was getting close to the end of the passageway. It was definitely getting lighter. He could hear Kayli's steady breathing and gentle splashes as she followed close behind. Quite suddenly, he was out in the open cavern. The lights were much brighter than the last time he emerged. He flipped over onto his stomach and paddled gently to his left to give Kayli room as she emerged.

Once Kayli was out, they both stayed as motionless as possible, floating just inside the entrance to the cavern. They could tell there was a lot of activity. Men were actually kneeling on the subs making adjustments of some kind. Others were doing some electrical connections under the giant monitors that showed where the subs were located. He did not see his father, but he did hear him on the far side of the cavern giving orders to some of his men.

"I think everything seems to be going as planned," Nathan said to Kayli. "It's time to meet my father."

Actually hearing Nathan say "time to meet my father" made Kayli very nervous. She had not been thinking about that aspect of this trip at all; she had been concentrating on how she was going to be able to act as a spotter. Now, it was time to meet Nathan's father and a whole lot of other people.

Nathan started swimming in the direction of his father's voice, and when he got past the first sub docked on his left, he saw him. He stopped swimming, and while treading water, waved his hand. His father spotted him, as did many of the other members of his crew. Everyone on the dock moved down to where the ladder was, ready to greet their visitors.

Nathan climbed out first and even though he was soaking wet, got a big hug from Jonathan. Kayli climbed out and stood on the dock rather awkwardly, waiting for the hug to stop. When it did, Nathan backed away from his dad and made some motions with his hands. Kayli had no idea what was going on, but she could tell Jonathan was watching his son intently. Nathan stopped using ASL and motioned with his hands as though he was presenting Kayli to the crowd, which he was.

Jonathan smiled. "Kay-lee? Is than correct?" Kayli nodded vigorously. Jonathan continued, "I wish our meeting could be under better circumstances, but that aspect is out of our control. Nathan has told us how wonderful your family has been to him. When this is all over, we'll have to have a big *luau*, but for now, I think it's best to get both of you to our house and into some dry clothes. Then, we can come back here and go over how we are going to coordinate our efforts. I think it will be important for you to understand what we will be looking at as we control the subs."

Using thalk, Kayli said to Nathan, "Can you tell your father how nice it is to meet him and to be in Hilo Dome? Also, I agree that we need to be coordinated in our efforts; it's just frustrating not to be able to make myself understood without an interpreter."

Nathan smiled. "Now you know what it was like for me outside my home. At least with my parents I can use sign language. That's how I'll be telling my father about what you are seeing when you are up on top of Coconut Island."

Jonathan turned to his men and said, "I'm going to take Nathan and Kayli to our house. We'll be back as soon as possible."

Nathan signed to his father, "We expect the attack to happen not tomorrow morning, but on the following morning. That's when they plan to knock out the generators. Then, they'll have to wait until conditions get so bad that the dome will have to open up."

Jonathan relayed this information to his team. Upon doing so, a nervous chatter swept through the group. Jonathan motioned with his hands for them to tone things down.

"Don't worry. You've all been doing great work, and we're ready for this. I can't speak for what is happening in other parts of the dome, but you all are the best. We'll get through this! Now, as I said, I'll get these kids home, and we'll be right back. Keep on doing whatever it was you were doing before our visitors arrived."

***

Jonathan found some clothes of Lora's that would fit Kayli, and he found some things of his own for Nathan. After changing, they headed back to the sub base.

On the way back, Jonathan took Kayli through the Lili'uokalani Park. She had never seen an ornamental garden like this, complete with ponds, streams, and gazebos. When they went to cross the Kamehameha Bikeway, she was astounded at the number of people on bikes. Kayli was also aware that several slowed down to take a long look at these two blond-haired teens. There were a few bikes in Honoli'i, but nothing like this. The density of the homes, shops, and offices was also unlike the openness she was used to in her home village.

Kayli was totally fascinated with the huge monitors and the electric lights. She had never seen or experienced technology like this before. However, after her initial wonderment subsided, she began to learn how Jonathan and his team of "pilots" would be controlling the submarines. Using an electronic map of the bay,

Kayli practiced giving locations to Nathan, who would then feed the information to his father. His father, in turn, would vocalize what the directions were and instruct each of his pilots as to how the boats should be maneuvered. After a couple of hours, Jonathan felt confident that they were a well-coordinated team.

"Let's go home and get some dinner," Jonathan said to Kayli and Nathan. "We can practice some more tomorrow, if you think we need it."

When they arrived back at the house, Lora was getting ready to prepare dinner. Jonathan had called her earlier in the day, telling her to expect two guests.

As they came in the front door, Jonathan said, "Lora! We're home!"

As she walked through the living room, Kayli rubbed her hands over the upholstered sofa and chairs. The protective nature of the dome and the houses preserved the furniture much better than what was found at her home. But the biggest surprises were in the kitchen.

Lora already had a chicken in the oven and was rummaging around in the refrigerator for some vegetables. She turned and shut the fridge door as they came in. She gave Nathan a quick hug and turned to Kayli.

"It is so wonderful to have you in our home. Please treat everything here as if it were your own."

Kayli said to Nathan, "Please tell your parents I am so thankful for their hospitality. In keeping with a name like Ohana, you have truly made me feel like family."

Nathan relayed this via ASL to his parents and said he wanted to show Kayli around the house.

"I'll let you know when dinner's ready," Lora said. "It shouldn't be too long now."

Nathan took Kayli to his room and showed her all his books and, of course, his guitar. Kayli said she wanted to go back to the kitchen to see how everything worked. They tried to keep out of Lora's way as she made dinner, but in the tiny kitchen, that was difficult. Kayli kept opening the fridge and freezer, not really comprehending how things were kept cold.

Jonathan watched her as she checked out all the appliances.

"There aren't many of these refrigerators left that still work," he said. "Some of my sub mechanics have been able to keep this one going. Of course, if Kawananakoa's men do what we expect them to do in a day or so, none of these appliances will work. I'm thinking we are going to need to learn an awful lot about survival without power from the people of Honoli'i."

"Okay, everyone," Lora said. "To the table; dinner's ready."

During dinner, Lora and Jonathan tried to learn as much as they could about life in Honoli'i. They also learned how Kayli and Nathan met, what Nathan's new favorite foods were, how Nathan learned many new skills, and what Kayli's family was like. While everyone was enjoying the conversation, Nathan was trying to decide whether to bring up some of his questions about how he came to be in this family, or not. He thought that just being here with his parents and Kayli was too nice to spoil with serious questions.

26
Readying the Troops

Kawananakoa and his force left Hāʻena and the flotilla behind. They made good time up to Keaau and quickly established their temporary encampment. Kawananakoa had some tasks for his men to accomplish so that they would be ready to execute his attack plan when the people of Hilo Dome were forced to open the panels. The main task was to construct spear torches.

While they had been in Hāʻena, Kawananakoa had directed his men to extract as much oil as possible from *kukui* nuts—fuel for the torches. His plan was to have at least a pair of his men at each panel. One man would be armed with a crossbow or longbow, the other would have a spear torch and would be armed with a *leiomano*, a club lined with shark teeth. The man with the bow would be positioned to shoot anyone inside the dome who was visible when the panel opened. This would provide cover for the other man to be able to light his spear torch and heave it as far as possible inside. Tending to any fires created would prove to be distracting and possibly create some serious air quality issues inside the dome. Each pair would be ready for either long-range shots or hand-to-hand combat.

Akuma Kuwabara did not stay in Keaau. As directed by Kawananakoa, he had to make his way to the encampment near the big waterfall just outside Hilo Dome. If this whole plan was to work, the ramming logs had to be ready to launch the morning after the main army arrived there.

Traveling alone, Kuwabara easily made it to the falls before nightfall. The man in charge of the ramming logs, Ron Osaka, met him on his arrival.

"I suppose you'd like to see what we have prepared," Osaka said. "I think you'll be pleased with the additions we have made to the original plan."

Kuwabara was curious. "Additions? Please lead the way. I'm anxious to see this."

Osaka skirted the buildings and brought Kuwabara to the river's edge.

"We have three ramming logs ready," Osaka told Kuwabara. "They are Australian pines, easily found all around here. As you can see, each one is about fifteen meters long and trimmed of all extraneous branches."

"Why do you have them here in the shallow water at the edge of the river?"

"After we cut them, we didn't want them to dry out too much," Osaka explained. "So, we decided to let them soak until we are ready to deploy them. They'll ride lower in the water and carry some extra weight, giving them a bit more punching power."

"What are all these logs?" Kuwabara asked, pointing to a pile of about twenty logs, each about two meters in length.

Osaka grinned. Those are our reinforcements in case the long logs don't make it all the way through to the turbines. Several minutes after releasing the long ramming logs, we'll send these out after them. Between the two different log attacks, we should really be able to mess up their turbines."

Kuwabara nodded in approval. "I really like the idea of your reinforcements. It's always good to have some back up."

Osaka said, "I guess you'd like to get some chow and a little rest."

"You got that right. It's been a full day's hike for me to get here."

"Come on with me," Osaka said. "I'll show you where our mess area is, and we have a small room set up in one the buildings for you to stay in. I must say, these buildings have made staying here very comfortable. I'm going to hate to give it up."

"I can understand that," Kuwabara said as they made their way towards the buildings. "However, I think you'll be even more comfortable when we move into our new residence, Hilo Dome."

***

With an attack anticipated in one day, Chief Teshima was spending all his time coordinating the dome's defensive efforts. He knew that, at some point, he would have to order the dome's panels to be opened. This knowledge came from times when Hilo Dome was forced to operate with only one generator online due to mechanical failures. Even with the air handlers operating at a reduced capacity, it did not take long for conditions in the dome to become unbearable. Temperatures soared, and air quality suffered. He could not imagine what it would be like with everything powered down.

He positioned groups of people at each panel. Each group consisted of someone who would have to manually open the panel by releasing a locking mechanism and then pulling the panel sideways on a track. Another member of the group would be armed with either a crossbow or longbow. Ideally, the third member of the group would have an electric pistol. Unfortunately, only ten pistols were charged and operational. In groups lacking pistols, the third member would be armed with knife, night stick, or baseball bat. Not the best situation, but it would have to do. It was all that they had.

His forces were spread very thin. Even though there were several thousand people living in the dome, half of them were children. The other half consisted of people too old for combat, people untrained with weapons, and lastly, those who were trained and able to fight. The only advantage Teshima could see that he had was that entry points to the dome were restrictive. As long as there was not a significant breech to the dome structure, there should not be an all-out brawl within the dome itself. He cautioned everyone to not go outside to fight under any circumstances. That would be suicide.

Jonathan Ohana had given him a briefing based on what he had learned from his son. According to what Nathan had told him, Kawananakoa was planning to gain entry mainly from the mountainside and from the bay. To keep temperatures down, though, Teshima knew he would need to open up all the panels, at least part way, so that the trade winds would be able to blow through. He would only be able to have one person at each of the side panels. The side panels had him worried. If the intelligence he received was incorrect, the sides would definitely be a weak point in their defense.

After checking with each group personally, he thought that perhaps he should inform Mayor Hapuna that everything was ready, at least as much as it could be. But then he thought, why bother? Hapuna was no longer a factor in how Hilo Dome was operating.

***

Jonathan, Nathan, and Kayli were back at the sub base making their final preparations. While they were there, they kept their eyes on the tidal cycle. Nathan and Kayli had decided that if the low tide was going to be very early in the morning before sunrise, Kayli could slip out then and not have to spend the whole night outside. However, if they figured out that low tide was going to occur after sunrise, they could not risk having Kawananakoa's fleet arrive before the spotter was in place.

All the subs' batteries were fully charged. Each sub could run for several hours on a full charge, but even so, Jonathan did not want to deploy them until Kayli relayed word through Nathan that the *waʻa kaukahi* were on their way. Kayli had said she would be able to see the canoes in plenty of time for the subs to leave the cavern and get in position. Jonathan had to take her word on this issue since he had never been outside.

They spent the rest of the day practicing their coordination with communication and piloting. It was all simulated since they could not actually deploy the subs without depleting their batteries, but everyone seemed comfortable with the process by the end of the day. After determining that the tidal cycle would permit Kayli to exit the dome a couple of hours before sunrise, they returned to the Ohana *hale* for some dinner and as much rest as they could get. Everyone was nervous about the next day, and sleep would not come easily.

***

Holokai Bishop and his flotilla rounded the point where Kayli and Nathan had turned back when they explored this section of the island. Bishop's scouts had informed him that there was a nice cove with a gently sloping beach area that would be suitable for bringing the *waʻa kaukahi* ashore and spending the night. As he surveyed the beach, he was pleased that his scouts were right. It was perfect.

When they came ashore, they discovered many of the *honu* that Nathan and Kayli had seen. Unlike Nathan and Kayli, who had simply enjoyed seeing all the turtles, Bishop ordered his men to slay and butcher five of them. He had them prepare the turtles for dinner, a little delicacy for his men to enjoy, as the rest of his crew set up their temporary encampment.

Also, unlike Kayli and Nathan, Bishop and his men did not notice the small footprints all over the beach. Bringing thirty canoes ashore with 120 men quickly obliterated them.

However, all the activity did not go unnoticed. The children from the little village had watched as the men came ashore after taking cover in the vegetation along the shoreline. When they saw them slaughtering the *honu*, animals sacred to them, and certainly something no one from their village ever did, they raced back to tell their parents about what they saw.

What the children described worried everyone in the village. They had never heard of, let alone seen, a grouping of this many men, men who would kill *honu*. After a quick meeting, it was decided they would abandon the village, at least for a day or two, to see if the men would stay or leave. They packed a few belongings, even the tethered goats, and moved to the shoreline on the opposite side of the point from the men. It was a smart decision.

One of Bishop's men discovered one of the paths leading from the beach and pointed it out to him. Bishop gathered a few of his men and headed down the path. It seemed more substantial than a path made by a *pua'a* or goats; before they settled in for the night, it needed some investigation.

Soon, they came upon the two old buildings and thatched *hale* that Kayli and Nathan had seen. They watched from the edge of the clearing, but when no one appeared in the village, Bishop and his men moved forward and began to inspect each of the buildings. It soon became obvious that this was a village inhabited by very few people. However, having people around made Bishop nervous, even though he could tell he had far superior numbers in terms of men.

After a few moments of consideration, he said to his men, "Torch the place. That'll send them a message to keep away until we're gone."

Although the men seemed reluctant to do so, they followed his orders, and leaving the two old buildings intact, burned the thatched roof structures to the ground.

They returned to the beach and settled in for the night.

***

Kayli, Nathan, and Jonathan awoke at around three a.m. to go over to the submarine base. Although they did not need to be at the base this early, Nathan and Jonathan felt that it was necessary to see that Kayli departed safely. Kayli was wearing the same *kapa* shorts and shirt that she wore when she and Nathan swam through the cave to get into the sub base. She had some more swimming to do tonight.

They rode bikes to the base under the light of a brilliant full moon. Kayli was thankful for the lack of cloud cover since she had to swim from the entrance of the cave around to where they had left their *waʻa kaukahi* two days ago. Then, she had to climb up to the top of Coconut Island to take her place as a spotter. It was not a difficult climb, but the moonlight would certainly make it a lot easier.

As they stood by the ladder that descended into the water at the stern of one of the submarines, Nathan gave Kayli a big hug.

"Be safe," Nathan said. "Hopefully this will all be over soon. When you get to the top of Coconut Island, send me a message to make sure our communication link is clear. I don't think there will be a problem since you will basically be right above where we are standing now."

Kayli gave him a squeeze back. "I'll be fine. We'll be back together soon."

Jonathan and Nathan watched Kayli climb down the ladder, turn, and ease herself into the water. They continued watching until they saw her flip onto her back and disappear into the dark cave entrance. They went over to the main control console and sat on a pair of stools.

Jonathan could see the concerned look on Nathan's face. "She'll be fine, Nathan. In fact, she is probably in the safest place in the whole area around the dome."

"As long as she isn't spotted by Kawananakoa's men in the canoes."

"You said there was good cover there for her," Jonathan said.

Nathan sighed. "Yeah, there is. It's just hard not to be worried."

They sat in silence for a few minutes as they fiddled with some of the controls.

Using ASL, Nathan said, "Dad, I have to ask you this question, and now's as good a time as any since it's just us."

Jonathan was pretty sure he already knew what the question was going to be, but he let Nathan continue.

"Obviously, I look very different from you and Mom and everyone else in Hilo Dome. But I *do* look like everyone in Honoliʻi."

His father nodded.

"So, I'm really having trouble understanding this. Shortly after I arrived in Honoliʻi, Sam told me a story about how they sometimes raid your *kāhala* pens and that normally it's very safe, but one time, there was an accident when the subs gathered the pens for harvest."

He stopped and looked in his father's eyes. Jonathan knew where this was going, so he felt that it was finally time for Nathan to know the truth, even though he had probably guessed it already.

"Let me start by saying, your mother and I wanted to have children very badly, and we weren't able to conceive the first time we had the opportunity to have kids through the lottery." Jonathan paused here, still looking his son in the eyes. "Because of this, we were allowed, by our laws, to try again for another year. Six more months went by, and we still weren't successful. Then, one day during a harvest, one of the subs came back to the base with a net that was in total disarray. All of us working there could see there was boat, a damaged *wa'a kaukahi*, caught up in it. The stern of the canoe was down under the water, twisted in the netting, but the bow was resting on one of the flotations."

"I directed my men to maneuver the sub under one of our cranes, in fact, that one right over there," he said, pointing across to the other side of the cavern. "One of my men jumped in the water and attached the grappling hook to the canoe, and we hauled it up on deck."

Jonathan stopped for a moment and reached out to hold one of Nathan's hands. "It was then that I got the surprise of my life, a surprise that changed my life and your mom's life dramatically, all for the better. Once all the noise of the sub and the crane operation subsided, we could hear what sounded like a baby crying, and it was coming from the bow of the *wa'a kaukahi*. We flipped the boat over, and there, up under the semi-enclosed area of the bow, was a little baby all strapped in nice and safe—very wet, but safe."

Nathan could see the tears welling up in his father's eyes as he told the story. He was, as he suspected upon hearing Sam's story, the "baby in the boat."

Jonathan said, "I took you home, and your mom and I decided that we would adopt you. We kept all this pretty much to ourselves; only my harvesting crew knew about you. Lora stayed home from work for several months using the excuse that she was having a difficult pregnancy. Of course, it wasn't difficult. We were overjoyed that you had come into our lives. We finally had a son!"

Jonathan and Nathan stood and embraced. Sam's story of "the baby in the boat" was confirmed. The thought that he might have been that couple's child had always lurked in the back of his head, but there was no way to prove it one way or another. Of one thing Nathan was certain: Jonathan was his father, and Lora was his mother.

"We thought we had lost you," Jonathan said. "And now, now you've come back into our lives. Not just as a memory, but for real. I never want to lose you again. I love you, son."

Nathan stepped back and signed, "I love you too, Dad."

As they stood looking at each other, both with tears in their eyes, Nathan got a message from Kayli.

"I'm in place. And that was really moving. Obviously, our communications are good; I could hear the whole story."

"Kayli's in place, Dad," Nathan said. "I guess now we have to get to work."

27
Attack

Alfred Kawananakoa and Akuma Kuwabara were already awake when Kayli slipped into the water to take up her spotter's position. They were down by the river just below the falls watching Ron Osaka direct his men. They were shifting the ramming logs from the shallows to a point where they would be ready to roll into the water. It was obvious from the way the men struggled that the massive logs were extremely heavy.

"That was pretty clever of Osaka to soak the logs," Kawananakoa said. "They should pack quite a punch when they hit the protective grating outside the turbines."

Kuwabara agreed. "I like his back-up log plan too. It should totally disable their electrical grid."

After about an hour of pushing, shoving, and using levers, the logs were in place. They were perched on a set of other logs that would enable them to be rolled out more towards the center of the river where the current was swift and the water deep. Osaka looked up from the river to where he could see Kuwabara and Kawananakoa silhouetted against the light of the full moon.

"Just say the word and they are on their way," he shouted up at them above the roar of the river.

Motioning with his arms, Kawananakoa shouted, "Launch!"

The holding pegs were removed, and the first of the ramming logs rolled down and into the swirling water. After a few minutes, the next one was launched followed closely by the third. Now, all they could do was wait and watch.

After what seemed like hours, but in fact was only fifteen minutes, they heard an incredible sound of metal grinding against metal, far louder than anything they had heard before except the deep rumbles from the volcano. They could see a few scattered lights on inside the dome. The ones on the right side flickered, and then winked out. The others remained on. At least one of the logs had rammed through the grating and found its way into the turbine blades.

Kuwabara shouted down to Osaka, "Half the lights we can see are still on. I think it's time to use your back-up logs."

Osaka signaled a thumbs-up and directed his men to send out all the smaller logs. This time as they watched, they had a better feel for how long it would take for the logs to find their target. Once again, they could hear the sound of metal against metal, but this time, all the lights went out. Hilo Dome was plunged into darkness.

***

Inside the sub base, nothing changed. They were operating on the stored power generated from the solar panels. It was a different story in the rest of the dome. Many people had been awake when the lights went out because they had anticipated the attack based on the information Jonathan had disseminated. One of those people was Chief Teshima.

Chief Teshima had established a communications tree. Each person who was awake and realized that something was happening had a list of people they were responsible for contacting. Once contacted, those people had a list of their own.

Lora was awakened by a knock on the door. She had fallen back into a restless sleep after Jonathan and the kids left for the sub base, but now the knock brought her fully awake. She threw on a robe and went to the door. Her neighbor explained that he had just received the word that an attack had occurred. As they stood on her front step and looked around the dome, it was obvious that the power was extinguished.

Jonathan, Nathan, and Kayli had taken all the bikes, so she quickly got dressed and half ran, half walked over to the sub base to let everyone there know what was going on. When she got there, as she expected, no one inside the base was aware of the attack. They were now. Nathan signaled Kayli to stand by; things had been set in motion.

Everything seemed to remain relatively calm over the next hour or so as people made their way to their appointed locations. No one was really sure what to expect next. For the moment, they were all safe since the walls of the dome were impervious to anything Kawananakoa could throw at them. They hunkered down at their stations and waited, weapons at the ready.

Far upstream from where Osaka launched the logs, there were others who were watching and waiting. Sam Pahinui sent word out for his people to stand by but be at the ready. They had all seen the lights go out, so they knew the attack was underway. They had taken their positions late yesterday and had remained in them overnight. It was a good thing they had done that. Even with a full moon, it was difficult to see well enough to move around in the forest.

***

Sitting on her mats and wrapped in the cover she had left, Kayli had the best seat in the house to watch the sunrise. The sun came up as a deep orange oval shrouded by a few clouds out on the horizon. They looked like clouds with no staying power, likely to burn off as the day progressed, giving no relief to the people of Hilo Dome. She shifted her gaze away from the sun, farther to the right, to the area she expected Kawananakoa's fleet to first appear. Nothing yet, but it was early.

The sun continued its relentless track over the dome. Conditions inside the dome continued to deteriorate, and Lora was helpless to do anything about it. By noon, the temperature had reached 120°, and it felt difficult to breathe. Oxygen probably would not be a problem since there were plenty of trees, shrubs, grasses, and agricultural plants to "scrub" the air. The humidity, on the other hand, was at its maximum. One hour later, Teshima gave the order to open the panels. The temperature had pushed past 130°, and the sun was still beating down on the dome. They needed air circulation desperately, and opening the dome was the only way.

Kawananakoa heard the creaking noise of the panels opening before he actually saw the panels move. It was the process of unlatching the door itself that caught his attention. Once he saw movement, he sent out orders for his men to light their small fires so they would be able to light their torches.

While this was going on, Kawananakoa directed another group of men to start a larger fire. This was to be the smoke signal to tell Holokai Bishop that the engagement with the dome was about to begin and to set sail from where they had spent the night. Once the fire was going, his men tamped it down with wet banana leaves, sending a huge column of dark gray smoke up in the sky. Kawananakoa was satisfied that it would travel high enough for Bishop to see.

Not far up the mountainside, Sam Pahinui and his force watched as all this unfolded. Sam figured the large, smoky fire was a signal of some kind, probably to the flotilla of *waʻa kaukahi*. What puzzled Sam were the small fires at each location where dome panels were opening. He had not been able to see the men there create the torches. He had no idea what was about to happen next, so he let his orders stand for his people to fire their first volley at Kawananakoa's men holding bows or crossbows. The threat they posed seemed to be the most dangerous.

The panels creaked open very slowly. Before Sam realized what was happening, Kawananakoa's men picked up their torch spears, pivoted around the opened panel, and while running across the opening, heaved the spears inside the dome. Too late to stop the spears, Sam gave the order to fire, and his people unleashed their volley of crossbow bolts and arrows.

At least half of the projectiles found their marks, and forty of Kawananakoa's best marksmen were taken out of the battle. The surviving marksmen and the club-wielding spear throwers were thrown into confusion. Startled by the surprise attack from behind and the loss of many of their archers, Kuwabara and Kawananakoa barked orders for their shooters to take cover and try to return fire. However, they could not find any targets. All they knew was that the attack had come from above them, and they were pinned down.

Inside the dome, Teshima's troops desperately tried to extinguish the spear torches. They were able to put out most of them, but all it took was a couple spears to embed or land near an old wooden structure. The tinder-dry wood of the buildings that had not experienced rain or any kind of moisture for over two hundred years ignited immediately and burned with an intensity that made each blaze almost unapproachable. The smoke was making it difficult to breathe as it billowed up and across the ceiling of the dome.

Teshima ordered several of his men to make their way down into the town to the hardware store and their homes to get as many buckets as possible. With no electricity, water could not be pumped to the conflagrations. They would be too late to save the buildings already engulfed in flames. The best they could do would be to form a bucket brigade to soak the surrounding buildings to prevent the fire from spreading.

With many of the Hilo Dome fighters abandoning their positions to deal with the fires, Kuwabara ordered his hand-to-hand fighters into the dome under the covering fire from his archers. He would lose some men in doing so, but it would be his best chance to overpower the dome fighters. The skirmish with the unidentified and unseen archers would have to continue outside the dome. This was certainly not the position he wanted to be in. He and Kawananakoa had envisioned a swift takeover. It was not to be.

On the first attempt, about twenty of Kuwabara's men made it inside unscathed. Some defenders seemed surprised to see them appear through the smoke, and the shark-tooth-embedded clubs of the men from Cook made quick work of the inexperienced fighters they encountered. Several of Kuwabara's men were taken down by Teshima and a few of his police force who were armed with the electric pistols. With more of Kuwabara's men arriving through the open panels, the fighting became more of a street fight with all the combatants using buildings for cover. The only thing that kept the Hilo Dome defenders from being routed was the inability of Kuwabara to employ his archers. They were pinned down by the force from Honoli'i.

Sam had to be patient. He ordered his people to shoot when they had a target. He did not want them to waste their ammunition in case this became a prolonged battle instead of a quick skirmish. Unfortunately, at that point in time, he had no idea how it would play out.

***

With the sun high in the sky, Kayli scanned the horizon. Finally, off in the distance, the first of Holokai Bishop's fleet came into view. She sent word down to Nathan, who acknowledged her message. He then passed the word along to his father.

Jonathan directed his pilots to take control of their subs. As they had rehearsed, the subs would leave the cavern in numerical order and take a position about one hundred meters from the entrance through the breakwater. It would not require much power to get them there and to hover in place as they awaited the arrival of the canoes.

Nathan watched the screens as the subs made their way out into the bay. On the screen, each sub was represented by a different color in the shape of a short arrow. A number beside each arrow indicated the depth of the sub with "0" being on the surface. As they motored out, each sub arrow had a "3" beside it, meaning the top of the dorsal "fin" was three meters below the surface.

From her position, Kayli could now see each of Bishop's warriors in their *wa'a kaukahi* paddling hard and in perfect synchrony as they raced towards the opening. She gave constant position updates to Nathan. The canoes were making good time.

Holokai Bishop was in the lead boat. He maintained his flotilla's position at about five hundred meters to the east of the breakwater as they traveled parallel to it. He spotted the opening, paddled another three hundred meters, and then turned to port. He maintained his position as the rest of the canoes took their positions. They would go through the breakwater five across and six rows deep. Once through the breakwater, they planned to fan out across the bay and land as simultaneously as possible. They were not expecting any defenders; they expected them to be very busy with their land forces on the other side.

Kayli described the formation and told Nathan the *wa'a kaukahi* were now just twenty meters from the entrance. When Nathan passed that on to his father, Jonathan gave the order to power up the subs to maximum speed. He wanted them to surface directly under the lead row of canoes, if possible, and then continue out to sea. Once Kayli gave the word that they were through the last row, they would make tight U-turns and head back through the breakwater.

Holokai Bishop felt the upswell developing before it hit him. One of the four subs surfaced directly under his boat, shearing off the outrigger and capsizing the hull. Three of the canoes in his row suffered the same fate. The subs, now fully surfaced, plowed through the rest of Bishop's formation. By the time they were making their U-turns, twenty of the thirty *wa'a kaukahi* had been destroyed. The remaining ten were in disarray. Some were trying to head back out to sea; others were trying to continue into the bay. None of them could understand what had just happened to them. None of them realized that the submarines had regrouped and, under Kayli's direction, were bearing down on them once again. The subs plowed through the breakwater entrance, taking out six more canoes.

Shattered hulls and outrigger parts littered the surface of the bay. Many had men clinging to them, while other men tried to swim to shore towards the beach where Kayli and Nathan had made their observations on the dome. Nathan relayed a message to Kayli, "My father is bringing three of the subs back in. If you still feel safe out there, we'll try to direct the remaining sub to destroy the last of the canoes. He will be piloting that one."

"No one is heading this way yet," Kayli said. "I'll stay with it out here and give you directions."

Once it became obvious which sub was remaining, Kayli began to send her directions to Jonathan. "Right ten degrees. Thirty meters ahead. Two degrees to port. Ten meters, five, direct hit! Three more to go. Come about 180^0."

One by one, the remaining boats were destroyed. The last two had no one left on board. Once they realized the sub was like a circling shark well aware of the location of its prey, they abandoned their craft and swam for the safety of the shoreline. Weaponless, tired, and defeated, they were no longer a threat.

After the last of the subs returned to port through the tunnel, Kayli left her position and returned to the cavern to be embraced and kissed by a happy but tearful Nathan.

"You were fantastic, Kayli! I am so proud of you!" Nathan gushed.

Kayli beamed at him. "We're a team. You and me, Nathan!"

Although he could not hear this exchange, as Jonathan watched his son and Kayli, he knew something special was happening right before his eyes.

***

Sam Pahinui's forces kept Kuwabara's archers pinned down. One by one, they were being picked off, and there was nothing Kuwabara could do about it. He was on his own at this point since Kawananakoa had left to find an observation point to see if he could assess how Bishop was doing with his attack. They really needed the reinforcements to come in from the bay and move through the city.

The fight inside the dome had slowed. The hand-to-hand combat was no longer raging through the streets. Several of Teshima's men with electric pistols had taken up positions denying Kuwabara's men access to the rest of the city. Teshima had also been able to reposition some of his men with crossbows up on the second floor of some of the buildings near the outer rim of the dome. They had been very effective at picking off any of Kuwabara's men wielding clubs before they could attack anyone. It was still a dangerous situation with no end in sight since Teshima had no way to assess what was happening outside the dome. He did know one thing. There seemed to be fewer men coming in from the outside.

The main thing that stopped the people of the dome from totally defeating the invaders was the fire situation. Too many people were pulled away from combat to prevent the fire from spreading. They had been able to contain the fires to the several blocks near the Wailuku side of the dome, but the damage was extensive, and the smoke had become a serious health issue. A hazy cloud had formed all across the top of the main dome. Even with all the panels open, it would probably take weeks to dissipate.

From a lava rock outcropping with a view out to the bay, Kawananakoa saw his dream of conquest unraveling. He knew they had been outwitted after they had managed to kill all the power to the dome. He did not know how that happened; he just knew it did. Now, as he looked towards the bay, he could see no flotilla of *waʻa kaukahi*. He was not sure what was actually happening down on the water, but it was becoming increasingly clear that no reinforcements were coming. He made the decision to find a weapon and join his men.

Slowly but surely, the fighting wound down. Sam Pahinui made the decision to slowly advance his people down the mountainside. Each team was to move one person at a time while the other three provided cover. If one of Kuwabara's men tried to shoot, he would be picked off. Shortly before sunset, Sam's forces stood directly outside the wall of the dome. His people had picked off six more archers, and the others had dropped their weapons. The fight on the outside of the dome was over.

Covering each other, they entered through the panels and took up positions where Teshima's men had once been in place. As they advanced, they were occasionally confronted with a club-wielding warrior, but they were dispatched before they could get close. Teshima's people positioned on the upper floors of the building saw them advancing. They had been forewarned that they might possibly be joined by the people of Honoliʻi during the battle. Their orders: do not shoot at anyone with sandy blond hair!

Finally, close to one of the still-burning buildings, Chief Teshima and Sam Pahinui met and shook hands.

***

Once the Wailuku section of the dome was deemed secure, Sam had his people join in with the people of Hilo Dome to extinguish the fires. Even though they could not talk with each other, their common goal was obvious. While moving along one of the bucket brigades, Byl came upon a body that looked familiar; it was Kawananakoa. He was on his back with an arrow piercing his chest. A shark tooth club was by his side. He let his father know that the leader from Cook, the self-proclaimed Kamehameha IV, was dead.

With the submarines secured at their moorings. Jonathan thanked all his people. While everyone was in a joyous mood, no one was certain what was happening outside the sub base. Jonathan, Kayli, and Nathan set out to find out.

First, they stopped to see if Lora was okay. All the non-combatants in Hilo Dome had been instructed to remain in their homes while the battle ensued. Jonathan was overjoyed to find Lora safe in their living room. After giving her a big hug, he asked, "What have you heard? Anything at all?"

"All that I know is that the temperature and odor of smoke increased throughout the day, but I haven't heard or seen any people in the streets," Lora explained. "I stayed put. With no weapons training, I would have just been in the way."

Jonathan, Nathan, and Kayli decided to try to move cautiously across town towards the Wailuku. They were concerned about doing so since they had no idea how the fight was going, and it was starting to get dark in the dome since the sun was setting. They had only gone a block when they encountered Chief Teshima and Sam Pahinui walking down Kalanikoa Street.

Jonathan thought, *Now there's an odd pair!*

Nathan and Kayli nodded vigorously in agreement.

"I take it everything went well on your end?" Chief Teshima asked Jonathan.

"Everything went smoothly. The subs ran perfectly, and Kayli was flawless as a spotter for us. She was very brave to stay out there when all the canoes from Kawananakoa were coming right in the bay."

Sam beamed at his daughter. "I'm really proud of you, Kayli!"

Jonathan looked at Teshima, covered with soot from the fires. "And on your side of the dome? Are we secure?"

Teshima nodded. "We are secure. We took some heavy losses, and many buildings were destroyed when Kawananakoa's men threw spear torches through the open panels. We didn't see that coming. However, if it hadn't been for the people of Honoli'i, we wouldn't be standing here talking to each other right now. We are forever in your debt."

Teshima smiled at Sam and extended his hand to him. Sam took it and gave him another firm, sincere handshake.

As he watched the two men, men who could have been enemies, now shaking hands in friendship, Jonathan said, "For Hilo Dome, it's an ending and a beginning."

Epilogue

One year after the battle, the people of Hilo Dome and Honoliʻi had developed a strong trade relationship, one that continued to strengthen as everyone involved learned American Sign Language. Sam Pahinui and his community had a lot of lessons for the citizens of Hilo Dome as they came to grips with life without electricity. The only power that remained was still being generated by the solar panels, but as before, it was dedicated to the submarine base *kāhala* fish farming operation. The panels could not generate enough electricity to power the rest of the dome.

All the ground level panels of the dome had been removed to allow greater air circulation and expansion of farming into the surrounding area. Housing would follow, but for the time being, the people of Hilo Dome were still cautious about moving out from under what now had simply become a giant canopy.

The people of Honoliʻi showed them how to harvest or catch the many kinds of marine life they had never had the opportunity to experience. It was important to understand what was edible and what was not. They also gave demonstrations on how to hunt *puaʻa* and to build *waʻa kaukahi*. Opening the dome had become a true awakening, an enlightenment, for the citizens of Hilo.

Roy Hapuna was forced out of office and died of an apparent heart attack a few months later. Andrew Sun was elected to be mayor of Hilo, and Lora was elected to the newly created post of deputy mayor. Chief Teshima stayed on as head of the police force, albeit one greatly reduced in size. Jonathan continued as director of the submarine base and was busy making plans to expand the operation using an outdoor port. This was one area where the people of Hilo could teach their teachers. The people of Honoliʻi were very interested in learning the art of fish farming in the open ocean. There were plenty of coves nearby that might be appropriate for an operation similar to the one in Hilo Bay.

Sam Pahinui remembered what Kayli and Nathan had told him about the tiny village they had discovered. He was curious to see if they had encountered the flotilla that came around the point on which they lived. He wanted to make sure they were safe. He sent Nathan and Kayli back to the village to see how they had fared and was dismayed to learn about the destruction of most of their buildings.

He quickly dispatched teams of skilled builders from Honoliʻi and coordinated with builders from Hilo to help with the reconstruction. He was not interested in incorporating the people from the small village into a way of life in Hilo or Honoliʻi; that was a decision they would have to make on their own.

***

Kayli and Nathan were married on the beach at Honoliʻi. Guests from Hilo and Honoliʻi gathered to watch them exchange their vows with Layla Pahinui, Kayli's mother, signing to the crowd. Everyone then returned to the center of Honoliʻi for a huge *luau* orchestrated by Auntie Bernice. She was in her glory watching everyone enjoy the food she had prepared. Contributions for the meal also came from many others in the village and from people in Hilo. Following the dinner, Nathan and members of the Pahinui family played guitars while people listened or danced.

Several days after the ceremony, Kayli and Nathan were making preparations to leave. As they had discussed, they were intent on exploring other parts of the island. Sam agreed to let them do it only if they took at least ten people with them, just as a precaution. Having their encounter with Kawananakoa taught them that not everyone might be as friendly as the people of Honoliʻi.

They were taking four *waʻa kaukahi*, each larger than the one Kayli and Nathan had used previously. They were not looking for speed; now they needed stability and room to stow things they would need on their journey. They gathered all the gear they figured they were going to need to survive and took it down to the *halau*. When they announced their plans and that they wanted others to accompany them, Kayli and Nathan had the difficult task of selecting who would go since they were definitely not lacking for volunteers. All the members of the exploration team were already there, packing their canoes.

The next morning, Kayli and Nathan stood with the rest of their team by their canoes. All their friends and relatives had gathered with them to say their goodbyes. Kayli hugged her parents, as did Nathan, then went down to the *waʻa kaukahi* to push it part way into the ocean. The other members of their team did the same. With their whole team standing in the ankle-deep water, they turned and waved goodbye.

Aloha, a hui hou!

Mahalo!

Thanks to my wife, Susan, for reading the drafts and making very useful suggestions in plot and character development. A special thanks to Jane McFann, for reading and editing an early draft of this manuscript. It's always nice to have talented (and patient) friends.

Also, thanks to my sister-in-law, Barbara DeFix, for reading very early chapters. I would send them to her, serial-style, and when I stopped writing in the middle of the story, she insisted that I finish it so she could find out what happened. Her voice in the back of my head was motivation to start again.

A special *mahalo* to Michael and David at the Kāne Plantation Guesthouse for creating in their Kanaloa Room a tribute to the works of Herb Kāne. His work in establishing the Polynesian Voyaging Society introduced me to the many styles of canoes used throughout Polynesia, and in particular, the design for the *waʻa kaulua, Hōkūleʻa*.

Mahalo to Rachel Millhone, Amna Majid, Diana Livesay, Dana Ungureanu, Dr. Kurt Brackob and all the people at Histria Books for accepting my manuscript and then working with me to make it better.

Other outstanding books for young adult readers:

For these and many other great books visit
HistriaBooks.com